C. A. M'Naughton

Sunshine and Shadow

C. A. M'Naughton

Sunshine and Shadow

ISBN/EAN: 9783744746878

Printed in Europe, USA, Canada, Australia, Japan

Cover: Foto ©Andreas Hilbeck / pixelio.de

More available books at **www.hansebooks.com**

Sunshine and Shadow

BY

C. A. M'NAUGHTON

Christmas 1885

GEORGE ROBERTSON AND COMPANY

MELBOURNE, SYDNEY, ADELAIDE, AND BRISBANE

1885

I INSCRIBE THIS BOOK

TO

𝔐𝔶 𝔐𝔞𝔫𝔶 𝔎𝔦𝔫𝔡 𝔉𝔯𝔦𝔢𝔫𝔡𝔰,

WHO

IN DEEPEST SHADOW, AS IN SUNSHINE BRIGHT,

HAVE FAITHFUL BEEN TO ME.

CATHARINE ANNIE M⁀NAUGHTON.

WILLOW BANK, ABBOTSFORD.
CHRISTMAS, 1885.

PREFACE.

 IND reader, after much hesitation, and in
compliance with many friendly requests,
I venture to place before you this small
volume of my writings. Its merits (if
any) I leave to your judgment. Wishing
you the Season's compliments,

I ask thee kindly take my simple lays,
(Remember I court not a " *Poet's Bays* "),
And in my scraps of simple rhyme I bring
In lines of love, affection—that I sing.
Chords inharmonic you will plainly see,
Expect to find no perfect harmony.
I know to some who read the lines I pen
Will come a dream of other days again ;
To some will come remembrance of a time
When life to them was like a " marriage chime."
To some my lay will bring a mournful spell,
'Twill tell of loved ones gone, of death's sad knell.
('Twill tell of faces missed, of voices still),
Yet faith will whisper, " 'Twas Our Father's will."

Somewhere a line of harmless mirth will show
That mirthful moment did the line bestow :
With *Christmas* and with *New Year's* greetings see
SUNSHINE and SHADOW blend for thee and me.
One thing suggests itself before I close,
Please gently deal with either rhyme or prose.

CONTENTS.

—:—

PAGE

SACRED READINGS.

CHILDREN'S PAGES.

SUNSHINE AND SHADOW.

CHRISTMAS!

WHAT sweet memories—what tender recollections of long years gone by—are borne to us again in that sweet, peaceful word, CHRISTMAS! How many of us who have passed the glad springtime of youth can in thought go back to our childhood's happy home —can again see there the father, mother, sisters, and brothers, with others whom we loved—meet in that dear old place to celebrate together the happy, festive Christmas-tide! Once more can we listen to the well-remembered voices, with their genuinely heart-felt congratulations, that were full of deep affection—once more feel the pure influence of that holy time—once more partake of the innocent pleasures with which that time was associated—can remember the fun under the mistletoe, the noisy mirth-making games, the true delight with which we drew the treasures from the Christmas tree, hear the shouts of laughter caused by grandmother

2

drawing father's slippers, father grandmother's dress cap, and one who was to be a future uncle a pair of baby's knitted socks: at Aunt Mary's drawing a cigar case, &c., &c. We were only children then, and our pleasure was not silent or our laughter subdued; we knew nothing of etiquette or manners, unless those which were taught us by purest affection, and the dear ones to whom we belonged were too well pleased with our enjoyment to unnecessarily restrain our mirth. But —there——. We can, alas! only review those dear days in memory; yet, whilst memory lives, such old kindred associations can never be forgotten.

GOD BLESS THOSE WHO MOURN TO-DAY!

Written on the occasion of the great disaster in a mine
at Creswick.

T this joyous, festive time,
    While we list to bells' gay chime,
    While the dear ones by our side
    Thoughts affectionate confide,
    While we see our loved ones stand
Clasping each the other's hand,
All at home—safe in the nest—
With no grief us to molest,
We for sad ones thus do pray :
God bless those who mourn to-day !

Whilst we whisper this our prayer,
Straying are our thoughts to where
Mothers with their children mourn
For their loved ones who are gone.
Oh ! what grief is theirs !—what woe !—
We can neither think nor know ;
But we pray that God may bless
Each and all in their distress,
And our words are, when we pray :
God bless those who mourn to-day !

Christmas, 1882.

TEMPUS FUGIT.

 IME is swiftly passing onward—
 Year by year rolls fast away ;
 Joyous bells will soon be telling
  With their peals 'tis New Year's Day.

Let us rouse, then—let us onward !
 Plenty we will find to do
In the year that is beginning,
 If we but the right pursue.

Be our station high or lowly,
 Duties new each day will bring ;
Let us see them when they greet us,
 Ere they pass on Time's fleet wing.

If we look around about us,
 Tears we'll find to wipe away,
Smitten hopes that we can brighten,
 Hearts to cheer with friendship's ray.

Let us start the year with boldness
  For to do "our Master's will,"
And at all times wrong evading,
  With His aid the right fulfil.

Let us labour nobly onward,
  Be our duties what they may ;
Meanest work, done with heart's service,
  Will the worker well repay.

With the old year that is closing,
  All vexations, cares, and strife
We bid good-bye ; and thus begin
  Again another page of life.

A PEACEFUL CONSCIENCE.

HAT are position, riches, fame, or name,
Without we have that which is best of
all—
A peaceful conscience? . . .
Can aught for lack of virtue compensate?
Can pure enjoyment come if we but take
The wealth of £ s. d., or titled name,
To gain us happiness?

And though our fame
Be widely spread, if we do not possess
Riches within, to cheer us and to bless,
What is that fame? To us it is but nought—
'Tis but a myth.

But if pure, honest thought
And virtuous feelings live within our mind ;
If we, in leisure hours, by self, can find
True happiness in thinking of past years—
Though oft those thoughts may bring affection's tears—
More blest are we, and richer far our lot,
Than he who wishes past could be forgot,
Though he has titled name or wealth untold,
Yet wanting *that* more precious far than gold—
A peaceful conscience.

NATURE!

OW blest is he whose greatest joy is found
In Nature's works! Above him, or around,
He sees the Mighty Hand—creative power—
That placed each star, that formed each tree
or flower,
That sent the ocean bounding on its way,
That made the night for rest, for toil the day.
He watches active ant or busy bee,
The bird that builds its nest in some green tree,
And, watching them, he oft will ponder how
God taught those things to work, made plants to grow—
Made sun to rule the day, the moon at night
To spread on earth its mild effulgent light—
Will view the valley and the rising hill,
And, pausing, think how vastly deep the skill
Of Him who planned it all : One Mighty God!

VALEDICTORY, 1885.

LD YEAR, good-bye! your pages are revealed :
The twelve months, which were yours, are
    past and sealed :
Old Father Time has had another score
    Since we our farewell said to Eighty-four.
And now, to us, there comes another year ;
Twelve vacant pages see with it appear !
And we must each and all assistance give
Those pages blank to fill. So may we live,
That by our ways and deeds, recorded there,
No needless blot may stain the pages fair.
May we for others try to do our best
(Man for his fellow man, with earnest zest,
Do what he can) ; and may we, day by day,
Have charity to aid us on our way,
So that when we the faults of others see
We may remember none can perfect be.
As we wish others our own faults to view,
With the same light may we see others' too.
May health, peace, happiness, attend our way
Till these twelve pages too have passed away !
May we be spared to see its appendix—
The seal placed by Time's hand on Eighty-six !

EARTH'S THINGS FADE AND CHANGE AND DIE.

EAR MOTHER,—I know all things earthly
must fade—
The flowers that live, both in sunshine and
shade ;
First bright beams of sunrise, that ope the
fair day,
With glorious sunsets, must too fade away.
Ambition's fond hopes, they will quickly, I know,
Fade fast into dimness, as we weaker grow ;
And all things around us—the bright, fair, and gay—
Will, like those less lovely, fade, change, and decay.
Likewise, we ourselves, darling Mother, must fade—
Must pass from earth's sunshine to dwell in its shade—
Must leave the gay scenes of bright Summer and Spring
To enter life's Autumn. How soon on Time's wing
Will Autumn be over !—and Winter, at last,
Make us wish that earth's storms and life's cares were
past ;
Oft, when frail and weakly, we wish it would bring
The last touch of fading, ere breaks the glad Spring—
The eternal bright Spring, the long, golden day,
That will not, dear Mother, fade, change, or decay.

*   *   *   *   *

Dear Mother, I know all things earthly must change—
Things once familiar now seem strangely strange ;
For loved ones are missed in our old house at home,
Some resting for ever, others given to roam.
Let me whisper, dear Mother, well you must know
Another is changing—to fade, and to go :
Your " Song Bird "—the pet name I once loved to hear—
Will no longer be " song bird " while she is here ;
The songs that I loved must be now put away,
The voice of the singer must cease its glad lay ;
Your singer is feeble, her voice it is weak,
With hardly enough strength sometimes for to speak.
The rainbow first changes its lovely tints,
Then fades into dimness, till at last it sinks
Away out of sight—so, dear Mother, must I
Change, fade out of sight ; but again, by-and-bye,
The rainbow will shine— will display just as bright,
Rare tints in its arched brow, on Heaven's blue height ;
The flowers that faded away with last Spring
Will freshly, next season, again perfumes bring.
Like rainbow, and flowers, hereafter will be
New season of life *never ending* for me.

*   *   *   *   *

Dear Mother, I know all things earthly must die—
Again in the dust all things earthly must lie ;
That my poor, frail body, and yours, too, must pass
Into the cold earth that is under the grass.
I must leave the scenes where I once liked to be—
I must leave earth's loved ones—they, too, fade with me—

For heaven's own bright glories that changeless are
 made—
For things will not perish, for things will not fade.
The flowers are fading, the leaves falling fast,
And, when the winter is over and past,
A form may be missed, a home-loved voice be gone,
No more to cheer or to sadden with its song ;
The singer herself will not then have the will
To sing you the old songs,—her voice will be still.

  *   *   *   *   *

Grieve not, Mother dear ; in the sweet "by-and-bye"
You will see me again, in that blest home on high ;
And, Mother, in Heaven, amid pure angel throng,
Far sweeter and stronger will be your "bird's" song.
Yes, Mother, I know we shall meet there again,
In that bright home above, where no sickness and pain
Will enter—where changes will come never more—
On a changeless, unfading, undying shore.

CHARITY.

Written to be read at an entertainment in aid of the Irish
Relief Fund.

DEAR FRIENDS, to us it seemeth well
   That proudly we our deeds should tell—
   Should show result of what we've done
   To help the famine-stricken one—
   To aid Old Ireland (dear old land !)
Whose brave sons well, with heart and hand,
Have toil'd for nought—have sown in vain
That which they could not reap again.
And while we speak of what is sent,
Let us thank God for blessings lent
To us—for gifts so freely given
By hand Divine from bounteous Heaven—
That we were able to relieve
Those sad ones in the depth of need—
That we were able well to spare
The needful, to remove their care,
Thank God, so freely from our store
We sent away to Ireland's shore !
And not alone to Ireland's sons
(In their distress, poor suffering ones)—
To India first we lent our aid,
Then China's cry came o'er the wave ;

To each we sent, and well we know
But duty did in doing so.
While means we send thus o'er the wave,
The distant starving poor to save,
Let us take heed not to forget
Those whose eyes with tears are wet
Amongst us here—whose children cry
For bread the parents can't supply.
Let us look well around and seek
The pallid lip, the sunken cheek
Of our own poor—and, when we find,
Also to them be likewise kind ;
That with a gentle, cheering word
(From heart with pity warmly stirred)
We will relieve their wants, and try
To soothe the mind, to dry the eye
Of weeping ones, who cry for bread
("Charity begins at home," 'tis said).

  *   *   *   *

Well know we there are even here,
In this our favoured land so dear,
Those whose thin cheeks might fattened be
By crumbs from our large charity.
So, while we work with heart and hand
To help the poor in distant land—
While gold and mercy, day by day,
We send to others far away,
We'll not forget, while it doth roam,
That "charity begins at home ! "

WATCH AND PRAY!

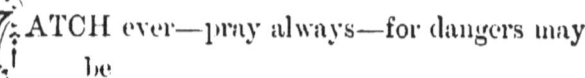

ATCH ever—pray always—for dangers may
be
Attending thy pathway that you do not
see ;
Temptations may wait thee along the
smooth way,
And sorrow be lurking where pleasure holds sway ;
So, wherever you be, watch always—pray, too,
That God may protect you and teach you to do
Those things which best please Him—watch ever to see
Your actions and conscience at all times agree.
Be certain, if fully in God you confide,
His care will protect you ; His grace, too, will guide.
In duties and pleasures, where'er they may call,
Watch—pray for God's guidance—He rules over all !

LOVING WORDS.

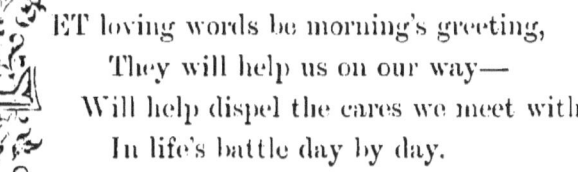 ET loving words be morning's greeting,
  They will help us on our way—
Will help dispel the cares we meet with
  In life's battle day by day.

Let loving words be evening's farewell —
  Words of love will sweeten rest,
Will bring to mem'ry, in our slumbers,
  True heart's affections, pure and blest.

LINES.

 EACH me, O Lord ! Thy will to know ;
  And, knowing it, Thy will to show :
In all my actions, give me power
To overcome temptation's hour.

WHAT IS, IS BEST.

 GAIN you speak about the past, and now
    You chide me that I broke a given vow—
    The vow I gave thee in the glad springtime,
    When I was young, and your strong love
        was mine.
But, stay! remember I was but a child,
With childish heart ; and you so thoughtful, mild,
Did win that heart through tender sympathy,
Unselfish love, and kindness shown to me.
You say that I deceived thee— did profess
To love thee, and replied with false caress :
I did not that (but yet full well I know
Thou wert too kind for me to treat thee so) :
But when you asked me for my love, and I
Consentingly to thee did give reply,
I thought it was pure love : so do not doubt
I felt within that which I showed without.
But after you were gone, and time had fled,
When quickly some two years had onward sped,
There came a day when I met one whom I
Did love with love so great, it could not die :
Not this, the childish love I gave to thee :
Not this, the love that came through sympathy

But it was woman's love, so firm and strong !
And knowing I should thee most deeply wrong
In giving it, I tried my best to tear
From out my heart this stronger love I bear ;
I thought upon thy love—upon the pain
That you would feel, but still 'twas all in vain—
My heart was his ; and so, at last, one day,
He asked my love, and what was I to say ?
I could not tell him he was nought to me,
Who was my world if I had been but free !

     *   *   *   *   *

What answer did I give ?   I told him all
The pages of the past I could recall ;
And he sat patiently to hear my tale,
To watch my tearful eyes, my cheeks grow pale,
While I entreated him me to forget—
To go away as though we ne'er had met !

     *   *   *   *   *

But, there—you know the rest—love won at last !
Come, say no more—let us forget the past ;
I am a happy wife and mother now—
My one regret in life, a broken vow.
You think amidst my joys and happy lot
That vow I made thee is almost forgot ?
But it is not : I ofttimes think of thee,
And that thy lonely lot is caused by me !

Still do I hope that one day thou wilt gain
Some loving heart to chase away each pain ;
That thou wilt win a loyal, trusting wife,
To cheer and brighten thee throughout thy life ;
That children dear may yet climb on thy knee,
And, looking in thy face, their father see ;
That I may hear thee yet, friend, when so blest
With wife and children, say—" What is, is best !"

A VOICE FROM THE BALCONY.

 WAS in the balcony, last Thursday night,
To see and be seen, and to watch with delight
The " Lords of Creation," who seemed glad to
   show
The ladies above them that they were below.
The *Host* of the evening, a most lib'ral man—
Who, when entertaining, doth best that man can—
Had gathered around him the——what ? Well you know
Trollope has told us that we often can " *blow*,"
So that I suppose I may say there each guest
Was fit to be present and mix with the best.
I can truthfully say I saw present there
Men holding positions that good men should bear ;
And also with pleasure I here wish to state
I saw many present both clever and great.
Of the banquet itself, I think I may say
The excellence showed itself many a way,
And nothing seemed wanted that money could buy,
Most fastidious to please and all satisfy.
Arrangements for ladies were, too, kept in mind
(Attendants in cloak rooms obligingly kind),
And, *en passant*, I think I need but to say
That caterer Clements did in his own way
Ad libitum provide for the ladies the best
And choicest of delicacies that thought could suggest.

Of the ladies themselves : many ladies were there
Who deservedly the name of lady can bear ;
But there were some who their rudeness must show
To persons their betters wherever they go.
But *parvenues* you meet at Melbourne Town Hall
If at banquet or concert or Mayor's dress ball ;
For when *ladies'* husbands hold positions of note,
Or (with plenty of *notes*) on position do dote,
They of course are invited, and think themselves great
When they show themselves little and ape the *élite.*
But enough of the ladies, and now I must tell
You Sutch's fine band played delightfully well—
The selections were choice ones, and after each toast
Tunes appropriately placed showed good taste in the
        Host.
Bowling prizes were shown, but the grandest and best
Was Dr. Beaney's own prize (admired by each guest) ;
It was won by a most worthy man of our town,
Whose good name is deservedly one of renown ;
For tho' much is known of his good deeds, I trow :
He does many kind acts the public ne'er know
(He is one of "*twa Kidneys,*" both of them good,
Who fortunes have made in abused Collingwood).
But I'm sure you will think, in my mad running rhyme,
Already I've wasted too much of my time ;
So I'll draw to a close—but just let me note
The "return" by the guests to Dr. Beaney, I hope,
Will be as successful as the event we recall,
Which took place 13th April in Melbourne Town Hall.

SONG.

" Always with Thee."

(For music.)

LTHOUGH from thee, my darling,
   I wander far away,
In fancy I am with thee
   Wherever I may stray.
Yes, always drifting homeward
   To thee, my lov'd, my best,
Is every thought that rises
   Within this faithful breast.

And if gay mirth surrounds me,
   If friends about me throng,
Yet still I see thee, darling,
   The first those friends among—
I see thee in some vacant place,
   Where I would have you be ;
And if I sing to please them,
   My best I sing for thee.

I think of thee at morning,
    When first I wake from sleep ;
I dream of thee at night, love,
    When wrapp'd in slumbers deep ;
And when sad thoughts oppress me,
    They waft me back to thee—
I need thee then to aid me
    With tender sympathy.

SONG.

"I think it would be Yes!"

(For music.)

ERE he to ask me when he comes,
    If I am glad to-day,
To see him safe at home again,
    From roving far away.
Were he to ask if, when alone,
    I someone oft did miss,
And he perchance an answer got,
    I think it would be Yes.

Or should he ask me if I thought,
    When he was on the sea,
About a certain ship that sailed
    Upon the waters free ;
Or if I prayed that ship would come
    Safe home, I must confess—
If I to him gave answer true—
    I think it would be Yes.

Were he to ask me if I'd take
A certain someone's heart,
And to that someone in return
With mine for ever part;
Or did he ask me if I'd seal
The exchange with a kiss,
I'm sure I could not anwer " No,"
But think it might be Yes.

AN "OWER TRUE TALE."

"Good-bye ! I shall be back at half-past five." . . . She little thought what detained him so long. That while she was waiting, he was sleeping the long, last sleep of death. . . . We deeply regret having to record the untimely end of two well-known and highly respected young gentlemen, which occurred through the upsetting of the boat in which they were rowing at the boat-race yesterday afternoon. . . . When the gate opened she ran to meet him ; but who could picture her grief when the sad sight of his lifeless body, carried by his late comrades, met her gaze ? She uttered one sharp cry, and sank senseless on the ground.

 WAIT and listen, listen and wait
For a hand to open the garden gate—
For someone to come with steps so light,
For someone to come with smile so bright ;
I wait and listen, listen and wait,
For surely my love to-night is late.

I sat and watched in the garden bower
After time we fixed full half an hour—
Mother called me twice before I came
To do her bidding. 'Tis now the same :
Instead of doing my work, I wait
To hear the click of the garden gate.

I wait and listen, listen and wait—
I hear mother calling, " Be quick, Kate !
How long, pray, do you intend to be,
Before you finish that seam for me ? "
I answer, " Not long," and yet I wait,
'Tween stitches, for sound at the garden gate.

My seam is done, but still I wait
To hear the click of the garden gate,
For my love to come with steps so light,
For my love to come with smiles so bright ;
I wait and listen, but all in vain—
Yet still I listen, and watch again.

    *   *   *   *   *

Ah ! how little we know—on Time's fleeting wing
The trial and sorrow an hour may bring.
He left us to go to that boat-race to-day—
So strong and so noble, so brave and so gay ;
One so well to be loved—'tis no wonder to me
That my poor girl is thus   .   .   .
                She expected to see
Him standing to greet her when she opened the door—
Excuse me these tears—I can tell you no more.

    *   *   *   *   *

I am over it now.   Yet the shock was great
When they bore him in through the garden gate ;
My lov'd one, my darling, did I wait for this ?
Not your step, your bright laugh, but Death's cold kiss !
But my darling lost !   Still I listen and wait,
For I know you will meet me at Heaven's bright gate.

A WORD TO MOTHERS.

HOW is it, at the present time, we find in the minority those women who are fitted to be good wives and mothers? Simply because, as a rule, young ladies are now brought up to think only of going out, dressing well, making themselves look attractive, and learning a few (sometimes not only unnecessary, but to them irksome) accomplishments, without attaining the far superior knowledge of household management, care of children, economy, cooking, mending and making, which acquirements all good mothers should try, as far as lay in their power, to teach their daughters. These, with a sound English education and the principles of *true* religion, are the really essential qualifications for making good wives, good husbands, good children, and happy homes. I do not want to depreciate accomplishments. Where there is a natural gift, by all means try to cultivate the same —that is, so far as it does not interfere with the required knowledge already stated. O Mothers! Mothers! if you would only teach your children to think less of the vanities of this life, and more of things that belong to the unchanging one which is to come, how commendable would be your exertions! how much more good would you bestow not only on your children, but on your children's children and future generations! Think of it, mothers; yours is a sacred duty. God has sent you children certainly to bring up to take their proper positions in life; but, at the same time, while you give them all the advantages you possibly can for so doing, remember your responsibility. Teach them this life is only one of short duration—given us not only to enjoy, but that we may so live in it that when it has passed away we may spend an eternal life in purest and everlasting felicity. Teach your children to know that it is not the outward beauty of the face, but beauty of the mind—not the grandness of the apparel, but the goodness of the soul—that will make them living lights to those with whom they come in contact; and that their good influence falling on others will surely, even here, bring its own reward.

THE LAST JOURNEY.

DEATH is the path we tread to meet once more
Our dear ones who have gained the other
shore—
Those friends that long ago from us were
riven—
True ones that loved us, we shall meet in Heaven.

LINES

Written on hearing a person speak of the failings of a well-known
public man after his death.

HUSH! let him rest! He's paid the last sad
debt
Of nature. All his mistakes, failings, now
The cold, dark mantle of the lonely grave
Hath covered o'er. Then do not, traitor,
throw
A hint of scandal. Mean, indeed, the man
Who dead one's faults so heedlessly can scan.
When one is living, it is base enough
Behind his back to speak a scandal's lie;
But when a man is dead, oh! let him rest!—
His virtues live, but unkind rumours die.

LINES.

O thee, who called my husband "much-loved
 friend,"
These simple lines of gratitude I send ;
Full well in many ways to me is known
Thy friendship was sincere—not words
 alone—
You loved my husband, and your deeds have said
What words refused to utter for the dead.
It would be vain for me to try to say
How thy true friendship cheered the orphan's way ;
How thy true sympathy did help to bless
The mother of those boys, left fatherless :
No need is there to tell the kindness given—
For know we such is registered in *Heaven*.

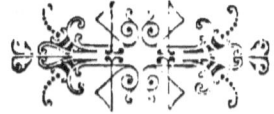

TO ——

18TH JULY, 1883.

THIS is the anniversary of thy birth,
  And many returns I trust you will see—
Long years may you be spared to cheer and
    bless
  All those who love you, and are loved by thee.

May Faith and Hope abide with thee alway,
  And every good and perfect gift be thine ;
May richest blessings still attend thy path,
  Pure friendship's light upon thee brightly shine.

I will not wish thee charity—for thou
  Art full of charity and kindly deed ;
Thy greatest joy seems alway to be found
  In others' pleasures, helping others' need.

I will not ask for thee one virtue bright,
  For all true virtues richly dwell with thee
But this I ask—thy sure reward at last—
  The Father's crown of immortality.

MAGNA EST VERITAS ET PRAEVALEBIT.

ET underhanded mortals blame the fire
That brightly burns in my outspoken ire—
I give them leave to do so. They may sneer—
Yet I will state my thoughts without a fear.
Outspoken honesty (though it be hot)
Is better than ill-will, that's spoken not—
Is better than the mean, degrading way,
Anonymously, some creatures have their say.
I know, plain speaking is a fault—but ween
I'd rather have the fault, and own my spleen,
Than be like some—I will not mention who,
Behind friend's back say things that are not true.

MIO AMICO! BEN' TI VOGLIO!

 HINK not that I can e'er forget,
 For always there will be,
 Within my heart, whilst mem'ry lives,
 A place reserved for *thee!*

Friend! still my friend! you this may know,
 Whatever be thy lot,
By her who shared thy childhood's hours
 You will not be forgot.

Perchance we all have need of blame ;
 Alas ! the world doth see
Most blame in him misfortune meets—
 So was it once with *thee.*

But now that fortune smiles again
 Upon thee, as of yore,
The world forgets that e'er it blamed—
 Folk praise thee as before.

Now friends (professed) thy way surround—
  Of thy rare gifts they tell ;
Know one true heart, in weal or woe,
  Still sighs : " I wish you well ! "

THE TWO WAYS.

 WO ways there be
For us to take,
As on through life we go :
One—laughter, mirth,
Contented mind ;
The other, naught but woe.

And if you choose
The better way
That is with sunshine blest,
You'll ever find
A friend that's kind,
And time for peaceful rest.

Should you prefer
The woeful side,
Then discontented be ;
Let little things
You fretful make—
Find fault continually.

Ne'er see the good
That others do,
Nor note the sunshine bright ;
But watch the clouds
That gather near,
Dispelling all its light.

So will you find,
If thus you choose
The darker side of life,
That very near
Will clouds appear
To bring you care and strife.

To walk the first
(Which is the best
You will with me agree) —
Wish not for more
Than is your store,
And ever thankful be.

See all the good
That others do,
And praise the good you see ;
Let love for God,
Who giveth all,
Be with you constantly.

LIFE'S THORNS AND FLOWERS.

 H ! well can I remember
  When I, a happy maid,
  Went tripping o'er the meadow,
  Or singing thro' the glade ;
  I had no thought of sorrow,
    My life was free from care—
  I dreamt not of the morrow,
    The morn was all so fair.

I thought but of the sunshine,
    And felt that life was sweet :
  I only saw the flowers
    That were growing at my feet :
  I did not heed the dead leaves,
    The crushed or trampled bloom –
  I only sought for blossoms
    That were fresh with sweet perfume.

I found, as I went onward,
  Along life's chequered way,
Weeds were mixed with the flowers —
  Clouds dimm'd the brightest day.
I found that there were sorrows
  In which I must take part—
That there was loss of kindred,
  Whose death would pierce the heart.

I've found that friends deceive us
  (Or those we thought were friends,
For sometimes folk are friendly
  To suit their selfish ends)—
That oft those whom we most love
  Can wound the tender heart—
That those we thought most constant
  From constancy depart.

Here so it will be always :
  We have our joy to-day,
To-morrow comes a sorrow
  That takes all joy away.
Our cares are thorns on rose-stems,
  Our joys the blossoms there—
And oft the stem with most thorns
  The choicest blooms doth bear.

I thank Thee, God, for blossoms
　That bud upon the stem—
I thank Thee, too, for sharp thorns
　That oft are mixed with them.
If life's stem bore but roses,
　I should not know the power
Of Thy blest consolation
　In sorrow's lonely hour.

But, with Thy grace to aid me,
　The thorns I'll meekly bear ;
For blooms that grow above them
　I thank Thee they are there.
I know well that hereafter
　No thorns will mix with flowers ;
'Twill be all joy and gladness
　Within Thy heavenly bowers.

LINES.

I F you would choice and lovely flowers grow
Within your garden, you must cultivate—
Prepare the soil—before you drop the seed.
So with the human heart.   If you would have,
In after days, it show forth wisdom's power,
You must from wisdom's store it well provide.

A BRIDAL ACROSTIC.

M AY health and boundless joy, dear maid, be thine ;
I ncreasing happiness attend thy way ;
L ight from above to guide thee—perfect peace
D well in thy guileless heart—throughout life's day :
R arest of blessings make thy pathway bright,
E arth's sunbeams playing round thee, with their light- -
D ispelling quickly clouds that dim thy sight.

S ince change must come to all, change comes to thee ;
N ow leave thy childhood's much loved home, and go
O ne other home to brighten and to bless
W ith thy sweet presence; and, in doing so,
D ear maid, friends many trust that you may be
E ncircled in that home, from sorrow free—
N aught but Heaven's blessing fall on thine and thee !

4

DAY-DREAMS.

8th March, 1885.

MY day-dreams one year backward glance;
once more I view in thought
That first night of my bitter woe, and to
my mind is brought
Again the scene where first I looked upon
his lifeless form,
With the raging sea beneath my feet—above my head
the storm—
I see the breaking billows, and I hear the ocean's roar,
That told me God had claimed my lov'd and best for
evermore ;
That told me he was silent, and his loving lips were
cold ;
That told me never *once more here* his arms would me
enfold ;
That told me his dear hand would smooth my tresses
ne'er again ;
That told me he had passed away, so painlessly from
pain ;

That told me he was absent—not the body, it was
   there ;
But the spirit had departed : it was gone—we knew not
   where.

    *   *   *   *   *

And, again, my day-dreams take me into a quiet room :
I see a bed of spotless white, on which are flowers
   strewn ;
And I see lying there a form, so peaceful and so still,
With a sweet smile on his features, and his pure brow
   icy chill.
His eyelids closed so gently, he seems in calmest sleep ;
Ah, yes ! to him 'tis calm indeed, but not to those who
   weep.

The scene once more is changed. I view a coffin and a
   pall,
I see it go—'tis all I see—and silence comes on all.
After it dawned upon me, that he would come no more ;
And then I felt this life was void, that all my joy was
   o'er.
I did not seem to understand that loved ones still were
   here ;
I did not try to understand they needed all my care ;
I knew it seemed in vain ; I strove to battle with my
   cross,
For my heart would only hear a voice that told me of
   my loss ;

That told me had left us, to see the vacant chair,
To miss the noble face that we so oft had gazed on
   there ;
That told me *never more* his steps would sound within
   the hall,
That told me *never more* his lips would answer to our
   call.
That told me all his love and care were only of the
   past—
No ! no ! it could not tell me *that*—his loving care will
   last
As long as this home doth remain—for, everywhere, we
   trace
Some memory of his thoughtfulness, which nothing can
   efface ;
Within the dear old place we see it everywhere we go
(Each wish we breathed was gratified, if he could it
   bestow) ;
We see it in things numberless, and, as we such things
   see,
We wonder why it is a loss like unto ours can be.

    *   *   *   *   *

O sad heart ! cease thy dreaming, if it can but dream
   like this ;
If day-dreams cannot show me faith, and hope in future
   bliss ;
If they cannot point me upward, into the life beyond,
'Twere better not to dream at all, if only to despond ;

If they cannot bid me look, and see, the teachings of
His love—
Who takes our dear ones from us, to lift our hearts
above—
If they cannot let me know His hand directs and shows
the way,
That leads me to a home of joy where friends pass not
away ;
That takes me to a changeless home, a home prepared
above
For those on earth afflicted, by *One whose name is
love.*
If they cannot teach me there are yet some duties to
fulfil—
Young lives to do my best for, while they climb life's
youthful hill —
If they cannot show me where to look for strength to
overcome ;
Then, heart, 'twere better you were still ! your dream-
ings all were done !

  *   *   *   *   *

Thank God ! above the weight of woe that day-
dreams bring to me,
His boundless mercies and His love to me and mine I
see ;
And though full oft my heart is sad—tears will not be
repressed—
Yet, through the sadness and the tears come soothing
words to bless :

" Child, fear not ! for I am with you, thy Father kind
　　and true.

I will not leave you comfortless ! I ever watch o'er
　　you !

'Twas for thy good I did chastise, hereafter you will
　　see

That not one sorrow you have known but what was
　　good for thee."

　　　　*　　　　*　　　　*　　　　*　　　　*

And sometimes day-dreams lift me, till I almost seem to
　　stand,

If not within, upon the verge, of " Canaan's happy
　　land ; "

And when such blissful thoughts as these across my
　　day-dreams steal,

Oh ! words cannot express the joy, the rapture that I
　　feel.

　　　　*　　　　*　　　　*　　　　*　　　　*

O Heavenly Father, grant that I may always trust in
　　Thee !

And that through all life's misty gloom Thy light of
　　love I see.

Oh take me, keep me, do whate'er it is thy will to do !

I only ask for strength from Thee to lead me safely
　　through.

I ask Thee, Lord, to keep me, to keep both me and
   mine !
I ask Thee, Gracious Lord, that we for ever may be
   Thine !
Both here and in the hereafter, oh, may we richly prove
That all Thy workings led us to the fulness of Thy love!

FAREWELL!

To the Rev. J. H. MULLENS, on his leaving the Incumbency of St. Andrew's, Clifton Hill, Collingwood.

AREWELL, dear friend! You leave us, and you go
  Regretted much by many; yet, we know,
  Although "in body absent" you may be
  From thy old flock, they still will think of thee—
Will ofttimes dwell upon thy teachings kind,
Will ofttimes bring those teachings back to mind;
Will think of how you taught a Saviour's love,
Will ponder how you bade us look above—
Bade us our burdens cast on Him who bears
For us our load of sorrow, sin, and cares.

     *   *   *   *   *

Dear Pastor, thou who hast true pastor been,
Think not thy labours wasted; oft unseen
Some seed did fall, and, falling, it did bear
Good fruit that did outgrow the worthless tare.

I know that I, myself, can truly say
Thy counsel oft hath helped me on my way ;
That by some words of thine a ray of light
Hath ofttimes come to cheer my cheerless night.
I know that others, too, whom I love well,
Regret as much as I to say Farewell !
That they, too, have been taught by thee to share
A Saviour's love more fully, and to wear
More openly their trust in His great power
To aid them overcome temptation's hour.

Farewell again, then ! May " the Master" bless
Thee ever, crown thy efforts with success ;
And if on earth our last farewell it be,
In Heaven above we trust to meet with thee.

LINES ON FLOWERS.

YOU tend your flowers with assiduous care,
Uproot each weed within your garden fair,
And well it pleaseth me each time I look
At such a cultivated little nook.
  Dear friend, my own true friend, I know, by
    thee
Deemed not presumptuous words I speak will be,
Therefore I tell you of some thoughts that came
Within my mind just now. You cannot blame
Those thoughts; and in expressing them to thee,
I do so fearlessly, though plain they be.
The thoughts were these : If you and I did strive
For flowers of grace within our hearts to thrive
As well as those which in your garden grow,
How much more worth and wisdom we would show !
Did we so cultivate our minds within—
Like you uproot your weeds, uproot each sin,—
Would we not let our friends more often see
The fadeless flowers—*Truth*, *Love*, and *Charity* ?
The flowers of *Kindness*, too, would bid us share
Another's sorrow, lighten others' care ;

The flowers of *Meekness* then would chase away
The stupid pride that we so oft display ;
The flowers of *Hope* would bloom, and blooming throw
Their fragrance all around each place we go ;
The flowers of *Peace* would anger oft subdue,
And *Self-denial* richly flourish too.
By faith and prayer, my friend, let you and I
Try to possess these blooms that never die !

ACROSTIC.

C ull choicest, brightest blooms
O ut of your gardens gay ;
L uxuriantly sweet Flora's gifts
L et us display to-day ;
I ndictive is our right
N ow proudly here to show
G arlands fair, plants most rare,
W hich in our city grow.
O trust we that great good
O ut of this cause will spring—
D isplaying Nature's works to man
  Must God to man's mind bring.

F air flowers ! ye can teach
L ife's lesson to us all ;
O ur lives are like your own—
W e live but for to fall !
E ach human life is even like to thine—
R emains to work God's will, then fades from time.

S uccess to Collingwood, and to its Show !
H. Walker long be spared the same to know !
O we we most thanks to him that we can boast
W ithin our city this an annual toast :

  " Collingwood Flower Show ! "

A SKETCH.

ISS SMITH?—Ah, yes, she called upon me,
    dear,
The other morning, just to have a chat—
To tell me the delightful time she'd had
While visiting her rich friend, Mrs. Hatt;
Engagements every night to party, ball,
She had (although six weeks she was away),
And with the grandest of the "Sydney swells"
She'd picnic'd, rode, or drove day after day!
Mr. Hatt, you know, he is immensely rich—
Drives best of horses, owns a mansion grand—
Keeps coachman, footman, butler there—ah me!
I never yet could quite well understand
How Bessie was so lucky— could you, dear?
I thought that I was fortunate when I
First won the love of Harold; but you know
His salary, though a good one, is not high.
Five hundred pounds a year is all he has—
It takes quite that amount for us to live!

I often wonder how you manage, Fan—
With children, too—on half that sum.   Forgive
Me what I said—although I know 'tis hard
For you sometimes—I did not mean to speak
About it, dear, 'twas just a slip of tongue ;
My tongue too often plays a foolish freak.
And Mrs. Hatt herself is such a dear
Delightful creature, always charming, gay ;
She dresses most superbly, wears the best
Of jewels, and her diamonds (by the way)
Outshine all others there.   She's quite the belle !
No party is complete unless she's there.
Of course the women envy her, and tell
Each other she was only this or that—
Her father was a tradesman poor, and she
Was no one till she married rich old Hatt.
Ah, Fan, dear ! when we three were girls at school
What friends we were ! we thought not aught could
        break
Those ties apart—we did not study then
Dress, diamonds, or the smiles of the *élite*—
I mean Bess and myself ; I know that you
Think no more of them now than when a child.
But then you have your children, we have none ;
You live so quiet, we *a little wild !*
Then Bessie sent no letter to you, Fan ?
'Tis strange she did not—but you do not care ;
She knew that Miss Smith and myself were friends,
And through that bade her me a message bear ;
She also sent a letter with her crest
Engraved upon it—Yes ! I have it here !—

Asking both Harold and myself to spend
A month with them beginning of the year.

* * * * *

[*A knock at the door. Cabman desires to know if Mrs.*
St. Clair is ready.]

Oh, dear! is that my cabman come so soon?
Then 1 must go. I have not yet had time
To tell you all the news. Will you and John
Come out to-morrow—stay with us to dine?
You cannot? Why? The children—always so!
Your excuse ever is the same. Well, dear,
Do try to come out soon—there—I must go,
Or else a scolding I shall have, I fear;
I promised to meet Harold on the block
At half-past four, and now 'tis quarter to!
So good-bye, dear; the children kiss for me,
Remember me to John—and now, adieu!

SONG.

(For music.)

FTER long grief and pain,
Say, shall we meet again ?
Meet where no more is sin,
Where sorrow goes not in—
To part nevermore ?

After the many tears
Shed through the waiting years —
Shed silently, unknown
(Unless to God alone !)—
What then will it be ?

Will it be our deep grief
Shall still find no relief ?
That we shall know in vain
Our sorrow and our pain—
That all, all were vain ?

Oh, foolish, doubting heart,
Within hath faith no part,
That you desponding say
Will sorrow last for aye ?
Our sorrow will not of a moment be
When once we gain joy of eternity.

ACROSTIC.

C LIOSOPHIC genius ! though he is no more,
H ow many are the minds that yet can be
A mused, instructed, by his labours past !
R are gift was his, for he had power to draw
L ife's every type of character, and well
E ach one was drawn.   By rich and poor revered,
S till will his name live on, though he be dead.

D rawn from his " Christmas Books " have lessons been ;
I n each we find " moral adorn a tale."
C an we read trials of " Jo " or " Copperfield,"
K ind-hearted " Nickleby," poor forlorn " Smike,"
E ndearing " Nell," but heart's best sympathy
N ew chords of pity feel for human woe ?
S miles suit thee best, not tears ?—to " Pickwick " go.

TO ——

On her Birthday. 10th March.

GAIN, fair maid, returns thy natal day ;
Accept kind wishes, which these lines convey :
And though devoid of merit the lines be,
Know—most sincere, the wishes sent to thee.
My wishes are—that best of all things good
Be with thee ever—may thy womanhood
Abound in blessings, and may purest joy
Be always known by thee without alloy.

May you be spared for many coming years
To cheer with friendship's smile, to dry the tears
And help the wants of poor, who ever find
Thy pity genuine, and thy spirit kind.
May you be like thy mother dear, and show,
Like her, the charity that she doth know :
The charity that makes her ever light
All those around her with its radiance bright.

Dear maid, I love thy mother well, for she
At all times kindness great has shown to me.

For that I love her—but I love her more,
First, for the love that she her mother bore,
The attention that she gave her, and the way
She cheered and blessed her, in life's closing day —
I love her character as mother, wife—
I think it perfect in her daily life ;
And, if but one thing I could ask for thee,
To be thy mother's self that wish would be.

"God bless you," dear one, on this natal day ;
"God bless you" always, thro' life's changing way.
If He his priceless blessings on thee pour,
We know we have no need to ask for more.

I WILL BURY MY SORROW.

 WILL bury my sorrow ; the world shall not
know
The tears shed in secret that spring from my
woe ;
I will hide it so deeply that others may say—
Her sorrow is over, 'twas but for a day !

Wherever I wander I find pain and grief—
I see many suffering who know no relief ;
Then blest is the thought—there is One, I know well,
To whom I my burden can silently tell.

I can tell it to Jesus, for He knows each care—
Each trouble, each heart-throb He taught me to bear ;
And ofttimes, when darkest doth seem the long night,
On Him well relying I find all things right.

He knows human nature —He knows the unrest
I have felt since He took from me him I loved best !
And He that doth pity will teach me to know
'Twas in love He afflicted, that in grace I might grow.

Yes, through my Saviour I always can find
Strength for my weakness and rest for my mind :
Not forgotten my sorrow, but each day I pray
I may gather the sunshine He sheds on my way.

I ask Him to help me (if 'tis His will
My life should be spared) His will to fulfil :
I ask Him to show me the way I can bless
My fellows afflicted, and help their distress.

I ask Him—poor, simple, frail one though I be—
That, by His strength helping me, others may see,
Whatever our sorrow, that Jesus can send
Consolation and solace—His love knows no end.

Hearts growing weary with weight of their woe
Droop 'mid the darkness.   Can I to them go
And tell them of comfort, if I let them say
My preaching, by practice I cannot display?

Oh ! may Jesus help me, by faith and by love,
To gather the blessings He sends from above ;
His sunshine unending, His truth it will light
The darkest of sorrows and make all things bright.

Possessing the gift, may He teach me to show
His light shining forth wherever I go ;
And may my lamp, burning, emit some bright ray
That will gild others' darkness and chase gloom away.

WHAT SHALL IT BE?

(In reply to a Letter from a Gentleman requesting an original
song.)

 SONG ! a song ! say what shall it be—
    Shall it be of sunshine bright,
Of clear blue skies, or of singing birds—
    Of morn, of noon, or of night?

Shall it be of childhood's happy hours,
    When you, a bright merry boy,
Thought all the world was full of flowers—
    Your treasure, some new strange toy ;—

Of the time you sailed your little ship,
    In the pond by spreading tree,
When you thought that ship a vessel grand,
    And that tiny pond, a sea?

Shall it be of home, where loving hearts
    Are tenderly pure and true—
Of those dear ones who, though far away,
    Still faithfully think of you?

Or shall it be of some flower rare,
  That you love to watch and tend?
And if not that, shall it be—but there—
  Say what shall it be, my friend?

Shall it be of deeds on battle field,
  Where noble ones are lying?
Of lov'd forms laid low thro' shot and shell,
  From home 'mid strangers dying?

I really know not—let me think again!
  Shall it be of storms at sea,
Of a sinking barque and shipwrecked crew?
  Friend, tell me, what shall it be?

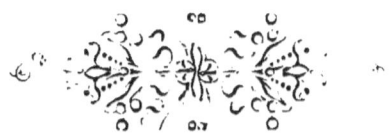

I COULD NOT, THOUGH I TRIED, FORGET.

THOUGH cold words for years did part us,
    Yet we could not strangers be;
Old links would not break asunder;
    Absence could not set us free.
Averted looks and glances cold
Did not chill the love of old.

I tried to teach my heart to think not
    Of thy winning, gentle grace—
Yet it would not learn the lesson,
    Time could not thy power efface;
For when I tried most to forget—
We were far less "strangers yet."

TO MY HUSBAND ON HIS BIRTHDAY.

1st JANUARY, 1884.

O thee, my husband, now upon this morn
    A double New Year's page will be begun,
    For with a New Year's light, long years ago,
    A babe you came—thy mother's first-born
       son.
And though so many years are past and gone
    Since first your eyes beheld the light of day,
Yet years can never make affection less,
    Nor Time cause love like mine to know decay.

What though are gone the youthful face and form,
    The fleetness of light step, which once were thine !
You are my ideal yet, the same as when
    To thee I first did give this hand of mine ;
And though, within my heart, for others live
    Purest affections, thou, amongst the rest,
Art always first, and truly well I know
    Of all my lov'd ones *thee* I still love best.

6

A WISH.

To ——

AY the new year bring thee
 Blessings from Above !
May kind Heaven shed on thee
 Peaceful joy and love !

May the rays of sunlight
 Brighten clouds for thee ;
Kind, true friends be near thee,
 Where'er you may be !

May thy heavenly Father
 Mark for thee the way
He would have thee walk in ;
 So that, day by day,
With His grace to aid thee—
 With His hand to guide—
You may fight life's battle
 Walking by His side !

This you may be sure of,
 What He wills is best ;
Only do thy duty,
 Leave to Him the rest.

SONG.

 AM waiting ! only waiting
　　Till summons comes to say,
I may go unto my darling
　　For evermore to stay—
May go unto the Golden Land,
　　The land of joy and peace ;
Where, re-united, loved ones know
Their tears and sorrows cease.

I am waiting ! and I know not
　　How long the time may be,
(There is one who in His wisdom
　　Permits us not to see
The length of earthly pilgrimage
　　Ordained for each one here) ;
But this I know, His hand will guide ;
　　Then what have I to fear ?

GOSSIPS.

T matters not to some weak minds,
　　Though failure may attend
　　Their tales of scandal, still they will
　　Molest each — so-called — friend.

If we would, when to us is told
　　A piece of *choice* " *chit-chat*,"
Treat it as though to us 'twere lost,
　　Nor ask the " *this* " or " *that*."

If we would try to stop the tongues
　　Of those who love to tell,
Without discretion in their words,
　　The things " they *know so well*."

Instead of list'ning to the tales
　　Which they to us make plain,
(And we make worse should we repeat
　　Those much-told tales again)

Far more commendable would be
  Example by us shown :
Could we but teach these Gossips that
  Their tales we quite disown.

Did Gossips try to study more
  Things good for them to know,
Instead of " *little-tattle* " tales,
  Much wiser they would grow.

But " little things please little minds,"
  And thus we plainly see
That persons who have little sense
  The greatest Gossips be.

TIME—PAST, PRESENT, AND TO COME.

 HERE was a time when life was sweet,
  When each fresh joy my mind could greet—
  When my young heart was full of song—
  When life, like rippling stream, went on !
  There was a time my spirit wove
Its fancy web of truth and love—
A time my step was free and light,
A time my eyes were gay and bright,
When they were not dimmed by sorrow's tear ;
But that time is no longer here.

Days of trouble and grief have come,
Smiles of joy from my lips have gone ;
On my brow are the marks of care,
Gray is mixed with my dark brown hair.
Times of anguish, shadows of gloom,
Dispel the rays of light that come ;
Through mist of tears I cannot see—
Flowers of joy bloom yet for me.

A day will come when earth shall be
A resting place, from sorrow free—

When this spirit shall know no care,
This wounded heart have nought to bear.
A day will come when from the tomb
I shall break through the mist and gloom,
In mansions blest I then shall be,
From all earth's pain and sorrow free ;
There I shall perfect gladness know,
Surpassing far all joy below ;
No tears, no partings in that home—
Thrice blissful time, when will it come ?

LINES.

IF we try to do the duty,
　　Which lies nearest to our door,
　　Do it well—without complaining—
　　Though it be but weak or poor.
We shall find, when it is ended,
　　Higher duties yet will come ;
And in each successive labour,
　　That is with heart service done,
We shall gather strength to aid us,
　　For to yet do greater deeds :
He who has true perseverance,
　　Is the one who best succeeds.

NEW YEAR THOUGHTS.

E are on the eve of 1886, and 1885 will soon be, like its predecessors, a thing of the past. How quickly the years roll by! We can scarcely realize that twelve months have passed away since we hailed the birth of the now-departing year; and yet, if we pause to think how many changes have taken place even in its brief race, we must see that it, like other years, has done its work, and brought to us all its share of good and evil. Politically, socially, and individually, changes come to each and all. Indeed, this is a world of change: with the years pass from us dear familiar forms—with the years pass from us intentions not fulfilled, hopes not realized, and labours (seemingly to us) spent in vain. Therefore, we may say of the old friend now bidding us farewell, it (like other years) has done its work—not, perhaps, to our satisfaction—not as we would have had it done, but according to that GREAT POWER "that doeth all things wisely and well." We will not minutely review the past; we have all had our cup of sorrow mixed with the draughts of this life's pleasures ; we well know that some have cares which joy can never heal,

and heart sorrows which will never be quite obliterated until the hearts containing them have ceased to throb : but for such there is "Balm in Gilead" and a Great Physician in time of need.　And now that we wish the Old Year good-bye, let us welcome the New with feelings of thankfulness for lives prolonged, and unnumbered mercies bestowed upon us by the Giver of all good ; and, whilst we make fresh resolutions for spending our lives better (should we be spared during the coming year), let us not forget to ask the aid of the Divine Being to enable us to fulfil our duties, and bear the trials with which we shall always have to contend while fighting the battle of life.　And, amidst all the pleasures that fall to our lot (may they be many !) let us hear the whisper of the "still small voice," so that, whilst enjoying the delights of this life, we may not forget the life hereafter, where time will have no changes, where years and centuries will be but as a day—that life which will be unending bliss, with no cloud or disappointment to mar its everlasting joy !

ACROSTIC.

(Written impromptu in the album of a young matron, who asked the Authoress to "dot down" some of a wife's duties in an acrostic on the word "marriage.")

M ARRIAGE! you ask its duties? Very few
A re those in "marriage" I can tell to you.
R emember, if good wife you wish to make,
R eligion, truth, unselfishness, you take ;
I n such, with true affection, sympathy,
A husband's lasting love secured will be.
G uide well thy household, from it seldom stray—
E arth's Home to man is where true wife has sway.

88

MY LOVE.

(A Valentine.)

HE doth not wear bright jewels grand,
 Yet she is full of grace—
For she hath tenderness and peace
 Both written on her face.

Her smiles are jewels bright and rare,
 Her words of gentle love
Fall on the poor, the young and old,
 Like whispers from above.

She doth not need a silken gown
 To make her look more fair,
For robes of purity and truth
 Are those my love doth wear.

She doth not need a jewelled gem
 Around her brow to twine,
For on her brow, so pure and white,
 Deep gems of thought do shine.

Her voice, like music's sweetest tone,
  Is full of melody,
And dearer far than wealth or fame
  Is that sweet voice to me.

Her eyes they shine with love's pure ray,
  Half earthly, half divine—
To me no other in the world
  Like this sweet love of mine.

WHY WAS IT?

DARK were the clouds, no moonlight fell,
No stars were glimmering in the sky ;
I heeded not the clouds, nor felt
The cold wind as it hurried by.
But as I went my lonely ride,
Right cheerfully I whistled one
Of Jessie's songs, for Jessie's smile
Was waiting for me further on ;
I heeded neither wind nor rain—
My heart was gay, and free from pain,
  When on the way to Jessie.

When I bade Jessie dear farewell,
Bright stars were twinkling in the sky—
Serenely, too, the moonbeams fell ;
The clouds were gone, no storm was nigh;
Yet as I went my homeward way,
The path I trod seemed drear and long ;
I was not cheered by moon's bright ray—
I whistled then no merry song—
Now, what was it that made me sad?
I know! I am a foolish lad—
  'Twas coming back from Jessie.

LINES.

(Written at a party on hearing played the air of a song sung by
my father when I was a child.)

HARK! what is that? A sound I hear—
A sound melodious, sweet, and clear!
It steals upon me like a dream
Of some almost forgotten theme;
And, as I list to the sweet lay,
Long-silent voices seem to say,
In gentle words, regretfully,
Oh! tell us, can it ever be
That old song which, night after night,
In childhood's home, gave such delight—
That old song, sung by him most dear
Whom we did fondly love, revere—
Can pass away in time from thee,
Forgot within thy memory?

    *   *   *   *

O lov'd ones of the past! within my mind,
In fancy now, I hear thy voices kind;

And once again I see that father dear,
And once again methinks his voice I hear :
That tune ! it is one which he used to sing
To please our childish fancies, and to bring
Us round the hearth (the hearth where was no care,
For purest joy alone dwelt ever there) ;
And as I list to this old, simple lay
That even now (though years have passed away
Since last I heard it) makes me shed a tear,
What visions to my mind's eye doth appear
Of childhood's home and hearts that loved us there —
Of all that made our young lives bright and fair !

*   *   *   *   *

The music ceases, and my thoughts must turn
To those around me ; but for long will burn
The sacred feeling that came rushing o'er
My heart, while listening to that song of yore.

TO MY DEAR FRIEND MRS. SADDLER,

On her Golden Wedding Day, 28th August, 1883.

 HE "golden" anniversary,
  Friend, of thy wedding day :
  Warmest congratulations
   To thee we come to pay.

We come, and bring thee flowers
  Of affection, love, and truth ;
We know you will receive them,
  As you did in early youth.

And though life's Autumn now is thine,
  Yet fresh within thy heart
The Spring's bright sunshine lingers still—
  'Twill not from thee depart !

This is our prayer, that Friendship's smile
  May still thy path attend—
That richest blessings from above
  Always on thee descend ;

7

And when earth's journey you have passed,
  Be this thy lot to hear—
" Well done, thou good and faithful one,
  Thy home is waiting here ;
Receive thy crown and dwell with Me
In endless joy eternally !"

BRIDAL ACROSTIC

And Wish.

(In the Language of Flowers.)

E ver with thee may "bridal rose" abound—
V isions of joy along thy path be found !
E arth's sunbeams shed o'er thee bright rays of light—
L ight that will quickly break the mists of night.
I trust that "myrtle" and that "olive" be
N ow and at all times found with thine and thee.
E ach year may "maize" and "straw" (unbroken) stay.

" S weet Sultan" from *true friends* to cheer thy way.
" T are" from thee keep, but "shamrock" ever dwell,
" E pidendrum" never bid thee a farewell !
" W hitethorn" I know that you will always bear,
A nd "daisy wreath" I trust you still may wear.
R ichly on thee may "crocus" fix its spell—
" T hrift" always ready be its tale to tell.

" H awthorn" attend thy path where'er you be ;
" O sier," dear Eveline, still dwell with thee—
O n thee may God His priceless grace bestow,
D efend thee with His care where'er you go !

ACROSTIC.

(Written by request of the Rev. W. W. Mantell, and read by
him at the Service of Song, entitled "Christie's Old Organ.")

C rouching at attic door, behold a boy !
H is listening ear doth catch with eager joy—
R emembered well by him—a tune he knew
I n brighter days, sung by a mother true.
S ay, what is it that stirs within his breast
T he yearning thoughts of "home, sweet home," and rest !
1 t is not want and cold alone that bring
E ach thought that rises. Angels whispering—
'S tay round about him, and God's message sing !

(O ur God doth truly make use of the weak,
L ow things of earth, to work for glory meet ;
D espise them not—His teachings—be thou meek.)

O ld Treffy lived within that attic cold,
R ich in possession of an organ old ;
G rief, want, and loneliness the old man's lot,
A nd yet old Treffy was not quite forgot—
N o, there is no place where God's love is not.

O ut of this story you may learn the way
R ightly to claim a " home, sweet home " for aye.

H ere see we Treffy's organ had the power
O f winning Treffy kindness in an hour
M ost needed by him ; likewise Christie knew
E arth's brightest blessings through that organ, too.

S trange are the ways of Providence ! but view
W isdom of God, how brightly it shines through
E ach portion of this story ! Mark how well
E ach trifling thing assists God's praise to tell
T o you, dear reader, so be all things well.

H ome, home, sweet home ! Oh, may we all at last,
O ur journey ended, when earth's storms are past,
M eet there, to dwell upon that changeless shore,
E ngaged in praising God for evermore !

LINES.

(Written on an intended visit to my father's grave, when very ill.)

 WILL go to thy grave at the close of the day,
 When the bright golden sunshine is passing
  away ;
 Will take flowers, dear father, the rarest that
  bloom,
Affection's small offering to place on thy tomb.
(With the flowers will mingle sobs tearless that fall
For thee I so loved, whom I cannot recall.)
I remember thy goodness, I bring back to mind
That thy heart was sincere, as it ever was kind ;
And thy generous traits to my memory appear
Even greater, more noble, than when thou wert here.
I never forget thee, thou art always with me,
In sorrow, in pleasure, where'er I may be ;
Oft memory sees thee, as I saw thee when young,
" With a laugh on thy lips, and a jest on thy tongue."
Of this earth's pain and sorrow thou hadst thy full
 share !
For thy last years were full of bereavements and care ;
But, oh ! may our God, who chastised here in love,
Grant thee pleasures undying in heaven above.

I oft wish I could weep, but heartfelt grief like mine
Will not quiver with anguish nor " melt into brine ; "
And though merry and happy sometimes I appear,
Yet my burden's the same, the lov'd one is not here.
I will try not to sorrow—it may not be long
Before I, too, with thee, join the numberless throng
Of the spirits departed ; and, oh ! may we meet
All our beloved ones together at Jesu's feet.

SCRAPS OF THOUGHT.

SAY, what is death ? 'Tis naught, for death is
   not !
'Tis but the casting off of what impedes
     The spirit's flight
To gain that which will always be
Eternal life, unchangingly.

———

Do it bravely, do it well,
Whatsoe'er thy task may be !
If but lowly, let men see
'Tis higher made as done by thee.

———

'Tis only a little curl
   Of my darling's golden hair—
'Tis only a half-worn shoe
   That my baby used to wear.
'Tis only a small bone ring,
   With ribbon of faded blue—
But yet I keep and prize them all,
   As most true mothers do.

The little pattering feet we miss
Upon the household floor —
The morning's welcome, evening's kiss,
Will greet us nevermore.

If we would be truly great,
We must first be truly good —
Showing deeds of pity, love,
To our common brotherhood.

Deceit! what demon lurks within its power ?
What mischief can it work in one short hour !
What peace of mind, what trust can it dispel
With its dread curse no human tongue can tell !
No voice can tell ! No mind can comprehend
The sorrow that attends it. Friend from friend
Is severed by its touch, and by its dart
Is ofttimes broke a tender, loving heart.

ACROSTICS.

IN MEMORIAM.

HON. R. S. ANDERSON.

R egretted much ! – how much, words fail to tell—
O ur hearts in silence sigh a last farewell ;
B ut though from mortal sight his form is gone,
E ach noble deed of his must still live on ;
R emembered well by many yet will be
T he acts he did of love and charity.

S tatesman—one of the best Victoria knew,
T rusted by colleagues and by public too.
I t was his nature to work hard for right—
R ight was his watchword, shining truth his light :
L ife was to him to do the best he could
I n helping on the common brotherhood ;
N ot only intellect brought to him fame—
G ood, generous heart won for him honoured name.

A nd now farewell again to him we sigh,
N o need to feel ashamed, tears dim the eye ;
D eath's taken from us one we ill could spare,
E ach one that knew him must our sorrow share.
R evered and honoured, let the name live on—
S ince he is dead – of R. S. ANDERSON :
O n records of Victoria will remain
N o one regretted more than him we name.

THOMAS HAYNES, C.E.

T ime takes from us those whom we love,
H ow vain our tears to bid them stay !
O n Death's resistless wings they pass,
M id sad regrets, from earth away ;
A nd blest are they who, like to thee,
S afe in the arms of Jesus be.

H ence thou art gone ! In sleep's repose
A way thy saintly soul took flight —
Y es, dwells for ever where can be
N o grief or care to dim its light :
E arth's service to the Lord you gave,
S uch now thy God hath well repaid.

ANDREW C. LIVINGSTONE, M.D.

A nother dear one gone! One friend the less
N ow can I claim of those who did me bless.
D eath seems of late to come with eager hand,
R emoving my best loved to spirit land :
E arth's chain is growing short—the links are few
W hich now remain to me of tried and true.

L et abler pens than mine his virtues tell,
I only write acrostic in farewell.
V ain is regret ; yet felt regret must be,
I know, for loss of one so loved as he.
N ow his earth's duties, nobly done are o'er,
G od called him hence to dwell on brighter shore.
S ay, was it not (God's will is always) best
T hat he should find his well and long-earned rest ?
O ne who, as daughters love, did him revere,
N ow sheds for him the tributary tear :
E ver to her his memory will be dear.

LEONARD TERRY.

(To Mrs. Terry.)

L et one who knows thy anguish at this time
E xpress her sympathy with thee and thine ;
O ne who herself the same deep pangs hath known,
N ow felt by thee—left "desolate and lone."
A nd, whilst she would in worthless line express
R egret and sorrow in thy deep distress,
D eem not amiss her prayer that God thee bless.

'T is hard indeed ! but yet 'tis those we see
E ndowed with talents rare, with virtues kind,
R emoved are first away from useful sphere,
R egretted much by those they leave behind ;
Y et God knows best—we loss, they gain, do find.

RIGHT HON. G. S. NOTTAGE.

(Late Lord Mayor of London.   Born 10th November, 1823 ;
died 11th April, 1885.   *" A man greatly beloved."*)

G od knows at all times what for man is best—
E arth's triumphs, pleasures, sorrows, toil, or rest ;
O f His strange dealings we cannot know now—
R eserved for Him hereafter these to show.
G reat honours oft He gives to man, yet see
E arth's glories fade and man must lifeless be !

S ix months only since he whom now we mourn,
W ith " robes of office " did himself adorn ;
A ccipient of honour, to be proud,
N ow waits to-day a coffin and a shroud.

N ot world's position, pomp, or riches keep
O ne human being exempt from death's cold sleep.
T ake, then, all such away, but leave behind
T he honest name, the truth, and virtues kind ;
A nd, while a line in memory we pen,
G o, take a lesson, pause, and truly ken—
E ach one must go the way of mortal men.

IN MEMORIAM.

(Died 18th December, 1882 ; aged 75 years.)

 E, whose great love exceedeth ours,
Hath gently borne away
His child unto the changeless home
Of everlasting day.

For her the time of peace hath come—
The endless Christmas-tide !
She fully shares her Saviour's love
Among the sanctified.

IN MEMORIAM.

(My dearly beloved father, John Crane Nottage. Born 1st
March, 1821 ; died 13th October, 1870. *" To live in hearts
that love is not to die."*)

OW closed for ever are those truthful eyes,
 Those lips from which such loving words
  came forth
 Are silent now !
 And that expressive, intellectual brow
Is cold as marble ! still, I'll not repine,
For He, whom thou did trust, I trust in still ;
And know 'tis best, since 'twas His gracious will
To call thee hence, that thou should'st hence depart—
Depart to be at rest on other shore,
Where disappointments will not grieve thee more.

THE REASON WHY?

(A Temperance Essay.)

 CHRISTIAN clergyman and my brother were walking together, when they met a dirty, bare-footed little girl, carrying a bottle filled with beer. After drawing my brother's attention to the child, the clergyman pointed to the bottle, and remarked : "That is the reason, my friend, why that child must go bare-footed." *That is the reason.'* To-day my brother mentioned this incident to me, and, on reflection, I thought : "Oh, that I had the pen of a ready writer," and then I could write a "moral to adorn a tale" (as far as the demon Drink is concerned) on the subject of "The Reason Why;" but, failing my ability to do so, I will ask a few questions on "The Reason Why." The reason why there are so many wretched homes? The reason why fathers and mothers neglect their offspring? The reason why larrikins and larri-kinesses (so-called) infest our streets? The reason why there are so many useless, wasted lives? The reason why children have no love or respect for their parents? The reason why, in this favoured land, there is so much

want and starvation ? The reason why our gaols are
filled with criminals, our asylums with the afflicted ?
The reason why, instead of men, women, and children
having the love of God in their hearts, they are the
children of Satan ? In nine cases out of ten, if a truthful answer is given, it will be : Because of that fearful
evil, intoxicating drink !

Oh ! you fathers ! who only spend a little of your
earnings at the bar of a public-house, think what blessings these small sums would buy your children that they
do not now possess. You who squander a good deal of
your wages, who envy a steady fellow-workman his
success—pause, think that but for the demon Drink
your children might be as well dressed as your neigh-
bour's, your home as comfortable as his. And, oh !
fathers—husbands—not only think of money wasted and
comforts lost, but think—deeply think—of your wives'
almost broken hearts, of your children's sorrowful days
and unhappy nights, through knowing—what ? *" Father
is on the drink ! "* Ah, more deeply think that
you are wasting not only your own, but the health
and lives of those belonging to you. And, *most
deeply*, think that, if you do not desist, you are on
the path to ruin ; for, though God is merciful, and
ever waiting to welcome the sinner if he will but
come to Him, yet He has without doubt said, " The
drunkard shall not enter heaven." And you, wives,
who have the responsible duties of motherhood upon
you, never allow your dear little ones reason to say or
to know that their mother is the worse for drink. If it
is a dreadful thing for a man to be tipsy, it is ten times

worse for one possessing the name of woman; though your husband may be in the habit of imbibing too freely, *you*, following his example, will only make the ruin of him, yourself, and family doubly sure.

I would here ask leave to say a word to those who are in the habit of allowing their children to have "just a taste." It may be a taste of beer at dinner-time, or a taste of wine when visitors are present; but, in whatever way given, mothers, think that that taste, that little drop, may be the first step to your darling's ruin. If in other years that child—your child—should be led into evil through the sin of intemperance, he would very likely blame you—his own mother—for the misery he was obliged to undergo. Why blame you? Simply by the taste you had so often given him in his childhood's days, he had acquired a liking, in the first place, for that which afterwards proved his ruin. From the *taste* he had taken the first *glass*, from that glass the first *bottle*, and so on until he had become a *slave*— a *slave* of the *worst of taskmasters*, intoxicating drink.

We are all filled with anxiety and fear at even the prospect of war disturbing our peaceful land. We do not see that there is already going on in our midst (as well as in nearly every part of the world) a general war. I mean the war of Temperance *versus* Drink; and although I fear it will be a long time before the former is victorious, yet, unfortunately, do we see those attached to the enemy falling around us nearly every way we turn; whereas, if they would only desert their traitor-ruler and join the armies that Temperance leads onward, they would, instead of falling, not only be conquerors themselves, but perhaps lead many from the ranks of the enemy, and each of those thus led from the hostile foe, persuading others to join their side, would so swell the ranks of Temperance, that, even against the deadly weapons drink may use in its own cause, Temperance would, conquering, go on to conquer, until at last victorious it must be.

[The two following pieces were written (by request) for the Rev. W. W. Mantell, to introduce at the Service of Song entitled "Jessica's First Prayer."]

JESSICA'S SOLILOQUY.

HE people are coming for coffee,
  So I must stand silently by ;
I must not look at them greedy like,
  Nor yet let them once see me cry.
J know that I feel cold and hungry,
  I would like some warm coffee and bun,
But if I should once let them know it,
  They would say to me "Off you run !"
So I will be very quiet like,
  And then they will not me molest.
Here the pleeceman will let me alone—
  'Tis something to know where to rest.
'Tis nice for them folks to 'ave pennies,
  Such good coffee and buns to buy ;
And then that new white bread and butter—
  How temptin' it looks to the "heye !"
I suppose they folks must be good folks—
  That they never drink beer or swear—

And that is the reason, I fancy,
   That they 'ave those pennies to spare ;
I wish, just for once, that my mother
   Would give me a penny, that I
Might come like they folks, " hinderpendent,"
   A bun and some coffee to buy.
I know mother ofttimes has pennies —
   It is with them she gets her beer ;
I don't quite right understand it,
   But to me it seems mighty queer
That she should buy beer with the pennies
   When it always makes her so bad,
And not buy bread, butter, and coffee—
   And buns, too — as makes folks so glad.
I fancy that all beer is good for
   Is to make mothers beat and swear,
And turn their children into the street
   To find shelter it matters not where ;
I fancy—if I could but find it—
   There must be a place you can rest :
And if I only knew where it was,
   To find it I would try my best.
I know some nice children 'ave 'ouses
   And mothers and fathers " wot's" kind ;
I 'specs them children are different
   To those in our " halley" you find ;
I 'specs they must be very good like,
   And clever—not stupid they be !
I 'specs they must be clean and pretty—
   Not "hugly," as mother calls me !

I would like to be clean and clever,
  If only I could know the way—
I 'specs some one teaches them children,
  And feeds them and clothes them each day.

*   *   *   *   *

The man he is packin' his dishes,
  So I can no longer stay here,
And I must away to the "halley,"
  I 'specs mother now wants her beer—
I wonder if she will 'ave some bread ?
  I do feel so hungry and weak ;
But, there ! I know if she 'asn't none,
  About it I dare not speak,
Or else again she will beat me bad,
  And turn me out in the street.

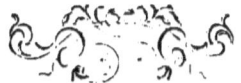

ACROSTIC.

J UPPON ! so ragged ! head and feet both bare !
E arth's lowest one ! no love for her to spare !
S ay, is it child like this of whom Christ said—
"S uch is My Kingdom !" This poor little maid
I ndeed seems sent no purpose here to fill.
C hrist knows His own—she yet will work His will,
A n earthly messenger that child may prove—
'S ent to lead others to a God of love.

F aith was in her first prayer ; and we may take
I ndeed from this a lesson : While we make
R equest to God, let us be sure that He
S hall answer send. If for our good it be,
T he answer may be given, and we not see.

P erceive yet two more lessons—let us try
R ightly these lessons to our minds apply ;
A nd what are these ?—One love ! one charity !
Y ou have but to possess them. You will see
E ach deed of love its own reward will bring —
R eal charity works good in everything.

TRUE PLEASURE.

YOU ask me where is pleasure found?
  I tell thee search the world around ;
  Have all that human power can give
  Have riches, titled name, and live
  On daintiest fare ; let luxuries grace
Thy dwelling-house in every place ;
And yet, though you possess all these,
They will not have the power to please,
Without you have within your heart
That truly called "the better part"—
The greatest blessing man can know—
The grace God can alone bestow.
'Tis but this gift can pleasure give—
True, genuine, lasting while we live ;
Such pleasure that will never fail,
But will at all times us avail,
And teach us so to live that we,
Thro' death, gain joy eternally.

TO ——

THIS is thy birthday, —— dear—
I wish for thee, from heart sincere,
That many birthday favours be
Now and all times sent to thee.
 I wish that you may richly taste
The best of blessings—God's sweet grace ;
And may His truths direct and cheer
Thee this and each succeeding year ;
May God at all times be thy Guide,
Whatever joys or griefs betide ;
And when this life is ours no more,
May we meet on a brighter shore,
Where griefs and sorrows come not nigh,
Where "God wipes tears from every eye"—
That place where all is perfect love—
Our Father's changeless home above.

LINES.

SIT alone in the twilight,
　　Musing on days that are fled;
And crowding into my memory
　　Come forms both living and dead.
When Fancy begins to wander,
　　She sometimes strays far away;
And oft I feel a child again
　　With merry young friends at play.
To-night, in my Fancy's dreaming
　　I saw my loved childhood's home —
Saw the well-known nooks and corners
　　There within its sacred dome.
I could hear sweet voices talking,
　　Telling, in their childish glee,
Their tales of innocence and mirth,
　　Beside a fond father's knee.
I saw the happy smile that played
　　And brightened my mother's face;
While she at work sat busily
　　In her own accustomed place.
I saw a tender little form
　　That sat close by mother's chair;
He was the weak one of the flock —
　　And mother's first greatest care.

I saw the happy, bright-eyed girl
  Of our household band the pet,
She whom we called our *Fairy Queen!*
  (She on whom our hearts were set)
And backward yet I wandered on
  To when I was younger still—
And with another sister played
  Beside the old water mill;
And there, the curly-headed boy,
  The brother I loved so well—
The one to whom I always ran
  My joys or my griefs to tell;
I see him, too!—Can see each one
  Of forms dear to mem'ry yet—
And well I know, while mem'ry lives
  I shall not one form forget!

    *   *   *   *

But where are they I picture still?
  Still can see with Fancy's eye?
Many of them are gone!—their forms
  'Neath the cold grey earth do lie.
That fairy sister is away,
  That brother, whom I loved best,
With mother's tender little lamb,
  Have all passed to perfect rest.
My father, too, though loved so well,
  On earth no more I will see;
But to a *Home* that changes not
  He will one day welcome me.

Blest Home !—Yes ; no more parting there,
　There no more a cross to bear,
No broken friendship, severed ties—
　No lost form, or vacant chair.
Oh, blessed Home !—oh, brightest spot !
　Where pain and sorrow will be o'er—
Where safe within the Shepherd's fold
　'Twill be joy for evermore.

LINES.

 LIKE a man to know his proper place,
I like a man to look you in the face,
I like a man in whom you well can trust—
One who will help your cause if it be just.

I like a man who, if he call you friend,
Is friend indeed—one who will you defend,
And, though to his own hindrance it may be,
Works manfully for you in charity.

I like a man who never will forget
The one who was his friend—who will not let
His own self-pride and egotism make
The friend look little for his self-love's sake.

I like a man, too, who will nobly show,
For others' sake, he will his own forego—
Know such a man, and you will have a friend
Who firm and true will be until life's end.

SYMPATHY.

 HERE is a Power that cheers the heart
    (It is the " Power of Love")
    That far surpasses pleasure's wiles—
    Its source is from above.

Sometimes earth's pleasures may enchant,
    But they will oft betray ;
And their vain smiles but lighten us
    To lead us far astray.

Yet there's a look, in kindness given,
    Makes all our grief depart,
And fills anew with brightest hopes
    The sorrow-stricken heart.

It stamps its signet in the breast,
    And, warmly dwelling there,
Will chase away the drooping thoughts
    That drive us to despair.

There is not here a purer joy
Than that affection feels,
When, 'midst the cares and trials of life
" It cherishes and heals."

For love's fond smile can shed a ray
So soothing and divine
That it will seem like beam of light
From some unearthly shrine.

Then let us scatter all around,
As we through life go on,
" Love's look," with cheering smile to bless
The weary, toiling one.

Let us shed sunshine on the way,
Though dark clouds hover near;
For ofttimes loving words will make
The darkest disappear.

AN ACROSTIC.

E arnest the wishes that we breathe for thee ;
D oubt not, dear friend, whate'er those wishes be.
W reathe health with joy, with peace, with friends most
    true,
A nd sum of blessings see we ask for you !
R eceive with these the prayer that *One* above
D irect and lead thee with His grace and love.

A nd this, thy birthday anniversary,
L et us try can we tune our minstrelsy ;
P oetic we would like our words to shine—
H ow well we know we lack both grace and rhyme ;
O ur wishes are to write a birthday lay—
N ot ours the fault our pen will not obey ;
S o take the wishes that we have expressed,
O ur few remaining ones twine with the rest.

T hough old the words, yet to thee we must say
H appy be many returns of the day !
O n thee, and on thy church at Clifton Hill,
M ay God vouchsafe His blessing.   May He still
A ddress thee with " *Fear not, ye little flock ;*"
S till trust in Me, the everlasting " *Rock.*"

9

TO MEMORY.

T is thy power which takes us back
   To other days that long have fled !
And brings again in passing dreams
   The visions of the lost and dead.

How often in our thoughts, once more,
   Alone amid the twilight grey,
A voice is heard, a hand is touched
   Of one who long has passed away !

And by thy influence we see
   Dear loving eyes, so bright and true,
Gaze into ours with tender glance,
   Just as of old they used to do.

'Tis by thy aid we think we hear
   The warblings, sweetly soft and low,
A loved one's voice to us did sing
   In happy moments long ago !

We gaze upon some relic old,
  ,'Twas left us by a father dear ;
And as we gaze, the tear-drops start—
  To think no longer he is here.

A little child runs past our door,
  With merry laugh, in noisy play ;
And mem'ry brings to us again
  A darling long since called away.

We join a merry, happy throng,
  Light-hearted 'mid that group we see
A form like one we still hold dear—
  From whence that pang? From memory.

Tho' sad sometimes 'tis to recall
  Dear ones are fled for evermore,
Yet with its sadness—sweet the thought—
  They are "not lost, but gone before!"

Not lost ! oh no ! again they come,
  And we, with deep affection, see
Our loved ones—still can claim them ours—
  By thy blest power, O Memory !

Thank God ! by thee we still may know
  The old bright smiles which now are gone ;
And that of loved ones we can say
  They live in memory ! still live on.

BRIDAL ACROSTIC.

E ver for thee, my friend, be love and peace ;
M ay joy and happiness with years increase ;
I n all the changes that your life may know,
L et friends be near to bless—where'er you go.
Y ou know my prayer, " God bless thee," I bestow.

T ime bringeth change for all, fair maid ; for thee
A change, I trust, where only you will see
T ime's change indeed was best. Now, dear, you break
C hildhood's loved links—leave childhood's home to make
H ome of thine own with him you love so well.
(E nriched that home will be with thy bright spell).
L ove be thy compass, dear, and may its ray
L ighten new duties—chase all clouds away.

[*The three following pieces were written impromptu, in reply to the songs named.*]

WE'LL SURELY "BIDE A WEE."

(Answer to "We'd Better Bide a Wee."—*Charibel.*)

YOU say I know the puir auld folk
   Are fading day by day,
And that I'm sure they'd miss you sair
   Were you from them away.
   You tell me times are hard wi' them,
     Of kine they have but three—
You could'na leave thy dear ones now,
   We'll, lassie, "*bide a wee.*"
You could'na leave thy dear ones now,
   We'll, lassie, "*bide a wee.*"

You say when first we told our love,
   They freely blessed us baith,
And did'na think o' self at all—
   They thought but of thy faith.
And, lassie dear, ye say ye ken
   Thy mother's "like to dee;"

You could'na leave thy dear ones now,
  We'll surely " *bide a wee.* "
You could'na leave thy dear ones now,
  We'll surely " *bide a wee.* "

And sad, alas ! ye say ye fear
  Thy father's failing too ;
Would, lassie dear, that I'd enough
  To keep baith they and you.
You know I love thee fondly, true—
  Love thine as well as thee—
So I'll not urge thee leave them mair,
  But, patient, " *bide a wee.* "
So I'll not urge thee leave them mair,
  But, patient, " *bide a wee.* "

LOVE'S GREATEST SPELL.

(Answer to " Then You'll Remember Me."—*Alfred Bunn, Balfe's Bohemian Girl.*)

HOULD other lips, however true,
  Breathe love's fond tale to me,
  It matters not though firm their vows,
  I still will think of thee.
  If in another sphere I'm placed,
Where prouder ones may dwell,
Yet there the tale I've learnt from thee
Will be love's greatest spell—
Will be love's greatest spell, love's greatest spell.

It would not grieve me though the world,
  Save thee, all false should be ;
It would not pain my heart to know
  That world was cold to me.
But deep, so deep, would be the woe,
  If you untrue could prove ;
Ah ! then, my heart would break indeed,
  That false I knew—ah ! false I knew your love.

I NEVER FORGET IT.

(Answer to " Out on the Rocks."—*Claribel.*)

 ES, I remember it, dear friend; I often
    Think of those days now so long passed
      away,
    When we two, light-hearted, roam'd by the
      sea-shore,
    Breathing our love vows in twilight's ray.

What did you tell me in one of those rambles ?
    What did I answer thee, " timid and low ? "
What promise made I thee ? Yes, I remember it,
    When " on the rocks, when the tide was low,
    When the tide was low."

I have not forgotten that broken, broken vow,
    Though I know you forgave it long ago ;
No ! I have not forgotten that old broken vow
    I made on the rocks when the tide was low.

I never forget it, but always think of it,
    When on the rocks if the tide is low,
If the tide low,
    If the tide, the tide is low.

SACRED READINGS.

SACRED READINGS.

"Evening, and morning, and at noon will
I pray."—PSALM iv. 17.

BEFORE retiring to your slumber, pray
That God forgive the sins done through the
day ;
And when again appears the morning light,
Thank God that He hath kept you through
the night.
But do thou more than thank Him for His care—
Ask that He teach thee of each sin beware ;
Ask that He give thee strength to do His will —
Your daily duties rightly to fulfil.
At noontime, when life's cares do thee perplex,
When things occur, perhaps, thy mind to vex,
Go thou to God in prayer, and ask that He
May give thee strength aright all things to see.

EVENING and morning, and at noontime, too,
From Him seek grace to lead thee all life through.

O Lord, teach me to know Thy will is best,
Grant that—I leave with Thee all things, and rest.

O Saviour, help me, that to Thee
Devoted all my labours be ;
From this day forth do Thou me guide,
O'er all my works and ways preside.

"COME UNTO ME."

"COME unto Me !" I know that thou art weary—
    That thou would'st fain lay down the
      battle's strife—
    That thou would'st drop the cross thou
      bearest now,
      And leave the mortal for immortal life !
"Come unto Me !" leave earth and all its trials—
    Leave disappointed hopes and tears behind—
"Come unto Me !" let Me but bear thy burden,
    And perfect rest thou evermore shalt find.

WHAT tho' the way is lonely,
    He is near—
He will protect and keep thee,
    Do not fear—
He will direct and lead thee
    All the way,
If only you will trust Him—
    Near Him stay.

His wondrous love unchanging it will last,
And still be ours when all earth's storms are past.

ST. JOHN xv. 4

I.

 NEED no other, Lord, but Thee :
If Thou wilt but abide with me—
If Thou wilt only let me share
Thy love, I then shall know no care.

If Thou wilt only speak, and say,
" Child, still my child, I am the way ;
Tho' weak and sinful you may be,
I will forgive thee —come to Me."

II.

O LORD, teach me to come the way
That Thou would'st have me—bid me stay
Close to Thy side, and let Thy power
Protect me in temptation's hour.

Let Thy grace guide and guard me here,
And lead me to a brighter sphere,
Where I shall ever dwell with Thee
Throughout a long eternity.

PSALM xxxii. 3.—PROV. iii. 6.

INSTRUCT and teach me, Lord, the way
　　That Thou would'st have me walk each day;
　　Oh, richly give Thy grace to me,
　　That I may learn and know of Thee
　　The paths wherein my feet should tread ;
　　For well I know that Thou hast said
To those who will acknowledge Thee
" I will ' direct thy paths,' and be
' A very present help ' in need."
O Lord ! to me be such indeed—
Be Thou my help 'gainst Satan's snare ;
In pain, temptations, trials, and care,
Grant that I hear Thy still small voice
Bid me at all times to rejoice—
Rejoice that I have always near
A Friend that ever is sincere—
The best of friends, my Jesus, God !
Who gave for me His precious blood.

"Cast your care upon Him, for He careth for you."

I.

HO knows the secret tears we shed
   In sorrow's trying hour?
Who knows what wounded spirits feel
   When by affliction's power
The heart is crushed, with none to share
Its bitter grief, its silent care?

With none to share—but there is One
   Who marks each grief we feel,
Who sees the falling tears we shed,
   And wants our griefs to heal—
A Friend is He who all will bear
If we but cast on Him our care.

II.

Doubtful one, why this unrest?
He who loves thee, knoweth best
What thy want, and what thy need;
He will not break the "bruised reed."

He in time will give relief—
Balm of peace for pain and grief ;
He in wisdom doeth best—
Cast your care on Him, and rest.
Though you think your pain and care
Sometimes more than mind can bear ;
Though you feel your griefs are great,
Pause a moment, contemplate
All the sorrows Jesus knew,
All the pain that He went through :
For us died—He knew 'twas best—
Cast your care on Him, and rest.

LINES.

I AM so tired, Saviour mine,
　I long for Thee to come
To take me to Thy golden shore,
　My everlasting home.
I know I have been wilful,
　Been oft by sin defiled ;
But this I know, my faith, Thy love,
　Will save Thy erring child.
O Saviour ! take me safely home
　With Thee, where all are blest—
Where sorrows will not try us more,
　Where weary ones find rest.

TO ——

(ON THE DEATH OF HIS ONLY SURVIVING SON.)

13th September, 1883.

FATHER ! of thy much loved child bereft,
What consolation can we give to thee?
How can we anguish keen like thine assuage,
Or help thee bear that which was doomed to
    be?
We know we have no power to lighten grief
Like that which thou art called upon to bear ;
But this we can do, pray that God may send
Strength from above to aid thee in thy care.
May He who knows at all times what is best,
Help thee to "Cast thy care on Him" and rest ;
May He, who "wipes the tear from every eye,"
Be with thee now, and ever closely nigh !
Be with thee always here whilst this life be,
And after this life closes may for thee
Begin that brighter life, without alloy,
Which will be one of never-ending joy,
When *you* will meet again (to part no more)
Your loved ones, who have trod that path before :
The path that takes us from this changing home,
To home where changes never more will come,
There re-united you again will be
To *wife* and *children* loved—eternally.

MY PORTION.

H ! to be wanting nothing,
 Only to sit at His feet ;
To learn the task with patience
 That He for me thinks meet.

Only a simple vessel
 Made fit the Master to serve,
That by His strength I never
 May from His precepts swerve.

Only to trust Him wholly —
 To know He doth all things well—
Only to see His wisdom,
 And have strength His love to tell.

Only to wait and listen
 To the teachings of His love ;
And, in those truths believing,
 Be made fit for *home* above.

Only be this my portion—
 Leaving earthly things behind—
" The mark of the high calling "
 In my Saviour Christ to find.

Rev. iii. 19.

HE Lord, He loves me, that I know—
For all His teachings tell me so
And earnestly for grace I pray
That I may love Him more each day.

The Lord, He loves me—Yes, indeed,
I see it in each time of need ;
And when earth's shadows darkest be,
'Tis then His love I fully see.

PARAPHRASE ON THE LORD'S PRAYER.

NOT only Father unto thee,
Or Father unto me,
But Father of the universe
Is God the One in Three—
Father of all who live or move,
A Father full of boundless love.

He is in heaven !—this we know—
But tho' His seat is there,
An omnipresent God He dwells
In earth and sea and air :
If in remotest place we be,
Our God is there our deeds to see.

O Father, hallowed be Thy name !
Let all the world adore
One God, supreme in majesty
Both now and evermore :
Throughout all realms Thy name be known,
And let all glory be Thine own.

We pray, dear Lord, Thy kingdom come —
 The time when peace will be—
When all who live upon the earth
 Will Thy great glory see—
" Thy kingdom come ! "   Yes, this we pray ;
Then hasten, Lord, that coming day.

" Thy will be done in earth and heaven,"
 So teach us, Lord to pray ;
That, whether joy or grief be given,
 We each in faith may say :
Thy will, O Father ! let it be,
For such I know is best for me !

" Give us this day our daily bread ; "
 Let bread of heavenly grace
Strengthen our minds and lift our hearts
 Till we behold Thy face ;
And earthly food do Thou supply
For all our needs until we die.

Forgive us, Lord, our trespasses,
 Incline our hearts that we
May rightly too forgive the faults
 That we in others see ;
And, oh, do Thou help us to say
These words with *truth* each time we pray.

Into temptation lead us not,
  But do Thou safely guide
Our footsteps through earth's pilgrimage
  Until we reach Thy side;
Deliver us from evil, Lord,
Help us to know and trust Thy word.

Thine is the kingdom and the power;
  All glory, Lord, to Thee,
We know alone is given now
  And evermore must be;
For ever and for ever, then,
Let all Thy creatures say—Amen!

A CHRISTMAS SOLILOQUY!

CHRISTMAS DAY!—the day on which we celebrate the birth of the greatest Monarch earth ever knew—the birth of the "King of Kings" and "Lord of Lords," our Saviour Jesus Christ. While keeping this day as one of pleasure and amusement, how many are there (even among ourselves) who wholly forget that it is the anniversary of the day on which THE LORD was born—or if not the anniversary (for there are many theological scholars who affirm that we hold the wrong day) the return of the day on which we think our Saviour visited this earth, to take upon Himself the nature of a little child, and to be not only a "Redeemer unto Israel," but unto the whole world—that is, to all in the world who will but put their trust in Him. Kind readers, accept my best wishes for Christmas socialities and Christmas pleasures. To you may they be many; but as friend speaking unto friends, allow me to say, while you enjoy all the happiness this earth can afford, may you (with myself) not forget to seek that higher joy, that peace which passeth all understanding—the "knowledge of our Lord and Saviour Jesus Christ." And may we all, trusting in Him, whether our lot be Christmas joys or

Christmas woes, know that by so doing we have a
" Friend who sticketh closer than a brother," who will
(whatever He sees best for us here) at last lead us to
that *Home* where will be unending joy and gladness,
such as we can never know until the *hereafter*.   Yes,

'Tis Christmas ! and I wish, dear friends, for you,
That joys be many and that cares be few—
That with this time of peace—" Goodwill to men "—
The best of blessings ye may richly ken :
Not only joys below, but from above
Be breathed to each their Saviour's new-born love.

"DEATH" AND "LIFE.

DEATH.

 REAPER there is who will not be still,
    He reaps at morn, noon, and night,
    Thro' summer, spring, autumn, and winter
      chill,
      He will onward wend his flight :
He visits the happy cottage home,
    Where the first sweet babe is given,
With only a touch from his ruthless scythe
    And that tender tie is riven ;
Father and mother are left alone,
Their bud is lifeless, its spirit flown.

Yet onward he goes, where a lovely boy
    Is the pride of household band ;
What anguish leaves there ! their darling is gone
    With stroke from his icy hand !
Then, away again, he must pause not here,
    For his work is never done.
Not far away is a maiden dear
    He would reap ere set of sun ;
He may not leave her, she is too fair,
Above she will bloom a blossom rare.

He never pauses—no matter the ties
    That may bind loved ones to earth ;
He still gathers on, and to those behind
    What anguish his work gives birth !
The father beloved, the mother most dear,
    He will them, too, bear away ;
But just one stroke from his sickle so keen,
    And they may no longer stay ;
For Death heedeth not strong affection's ties,
Sorrowing heart's anguish, or weeping eyes.

————

LIFE.

Although Death comes and bears away
    Those friends we dearly love,
He gathers for the Lord on high,
    For the Lord's home above.

He comes and takes the tender buds,
    The buds so sweet and rare,
To live in garden bright above,
    To bloom far fairer there.

He reaps the lovely, opening flowers,
    When bursting are their leaves ;
It is for Christ, their Shepherd kind,
    " He binds them in his sheaves."

And those he smites in youth's bright hour
  With his cold, icy hand,
He bids die here, to live for aye
  In Heaven's pure " happy land."

The ripened grain : those who have toiled
  And borne the burden long,
Are but released from earthly cares
  To join the angels' song.

Oh ! say not Death is stern and cold,
  Although to part is pain
(We know for us) from friends loved well—
  They life, joy, peace do gain.

They die—but to begin to live
  The life that never dies ;
They pass away from earthly sphere
  To mansions in the skies.

        *   *   *   *

Dead to a cold, unfeeling world,
  Dead to the thoughtless breast,
Dead to false friends (deceit, pretence)—
  From such they safely rest.

Not dead to those who loved : not dead !
  But only gone before ;
They live with us in mem'ry still,
  As in the days of yore.

Yet do they dwell within our hearts,
    And in our minds we trace
Each form we love (we hear each voice)—
    Behold again each face.

And while hearts with affection beat,
    While tears will fill the eye,
When thoughts bring back our loved again,
    They will not—cannot die.

 LESS me, dear Lord! and let me know
    All for my good Thou dost bestow—
Bless me, dear Lord! and let me see
    'Tis well, if I but trust in Thee.

STANZAS—NOT DEAD TO ME!

" The memory of the just is blessed."

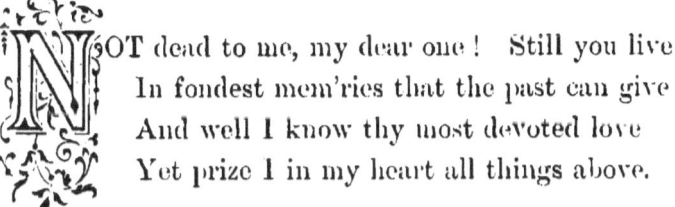OT dead to me, my dear one! Still you live
In fondest mem'ries that the past can give ;
And well I know thy most devoted love
Yet prize I in my heart all things above.

Not dead to me! I loved you far too well,
Whilst God permitted you on earth to dwell,
For ever to forget that 'twas but thee
I loved, as only thou wert loved by me.

Not dead to me! Each day, each moment brings
To mind thy thoughtful care—the many things
That thou didst do for me and for our boys,
The three with whom you always sought life's joys.

O husband! When I think, my darling gone,
Of thy great wealth of love so showered upon
Those children and myself—it seems to me
My heart must break with weight of agony!

If 'twere not for our boys, my darling, I
Would wish that I, like thee, might quickly die,
To go and dwell where there is perfect rest,
For I am sure that thou art with the blest.

But well I know these thoughts rebellious are—
That, if God wills it, it is nobler far
To strive to live, and try my best to do
To guide our boys life's youthful journey through.

*   *   *   *   *

Whate'er it be, I pray that God may keep
Our dear ones and myself until we meet
Again, my husband, on a brighter shore,
Where Death will have no power to part us more.

*   *   *   *   *

I know that I no longer look on thee,
    But on the cold clay house where you have been—
Where once your spirit breathed.   My farewell kiss
    I press upon those features.   Well I ween
That, though no more upon them I may gaze,
    Within my heart they ever *will* be mine ;
There will they dwell—no power bids them depart—
    Until it ceases beating like to thine.

*   *   *   *   *

Dead! Dead! Yes, he is dead! Say, can it be
That never more he may come back to me?
My own dear Alick, whom I loved so well,
With such affection that no words can tell
How much I loved him! . . .
O God! help me this bitter grief to bear,
And keep me in Thine own, good, tender care.

PATIENCE.

THERE is an angel ofttimes visits here,
  The weak, the suffering, and the sad to cheer ;
  And though we cannot keep from grief or
    pain,
  Or bring our loved ones back to us again,
Yet can he help us bear the ills we know,
And strengthen us to fight with pain or woe,
That angel—it is Patience ! May it be
Permitted, Lord, to visit mine and me !

CHILDREN'S PAGES.

CHILDREN'S PAGES.

— ❧ ✦ ❦ —

CHRISTMAS WISHES.

T this holy Christmas tide
May pure peace with thee abide;
Choicest blessings under Heaven
Unto each and all be given;
And may special joy be thine
At the coming New Year time.
Reader! I, thy humble friend,
Kind and earnest wishes send;
Merrie Christmas to you all—
Happy New Year festival!

THE JUVENILE INDUSTRIAL EXHIBITION.

 E'VE met to-day, upon this Eastern Hill,
To view the works of industry and skill]
That have been wrought with willing mind
   and hand
By Juveniles throughout fair Austral's
   land.
Welcome, kind friends ! we bid you welcome here,
For we are certain there's no cause to fear
Our Exhibition will fail to possess
Attractions great to crown it a success—
Attractions that will approbation gain,
To well reward the worker for his pain.
Rare works of beauty, novelty, and taste
Young friends have sent, our efforts well to grace,
And warmest thanks are due to each and all
Who kindly worked, responsive to our call—
To help us gain the triumph of this day
(For, is it not a triumph that we may
Justly be proud of ?)   Display'd here you'll find
Things that will please the eye, improve the mind—
Most pleased indeed we are our enterprise
Doth meet with such approval.   That surprise

We see depicted on each happy face
Now present, this our opening scene to grace.
But we must not detain you ; for to raise
Their voices high in anthem's song of praise
Our friends are waiting, and we know they'll please
You more with Music's lines than we with these ;
But yet, before we close, we'll wish to each
A merry Christmas, filled with joy and peace.
A happy New Year's time, kind friends, be thine,
Full of rich blessings sent by hand Divine.
Young friends ! We said, to you our thanks we owe,
And genuine are the thanks we now bestow ;
May you all strive with every bright New Year
Achievements more to win—still persevere
To mount Ambition's ladder, and aspire
By industry to gain what you desire.
May you work on with willing heart and hand,
Till Liberty, Peace, Knowledge rule our land.
Knowledge ! bright Knowledge ! may thy brightest ray
Drive all the clouds of Ignorance away—
Dark Ignorance ! Oh, may thy power cease !
God speed the cause of Knowledge, Love, and Peace.

THE GIFT OF ALL GOD'S EARTHLY GIFTS
THE BEST!

WERE you to ask me the best earthly gift
 That God could give to aid you here below,
A gift that would not fail you—would not change
  In weakness, health, in joy or deepest woe;
A something that would always hover near,
 To help you do the right, to shun the wrong—
To keep you truthful, noble, just, and good,
 To help you walk the narrow path along;
Were you to ask me this best gift for thee,
 A mother's love would, child, my answer be.
A good mother, my child! such the best gift
 That God can give thee here on earth; for she
Will train you for His service—she will lead
 Thee to His mercy-seat, and you will be
By her prayers blessed. By her you will be taught
 To put your trust in Him who keepeth all;
Will, by her teaching, know that He will aid
 With His good grace all those who on Him call;
And if your path should be where dangers lie,
 Her teachings will have taught you that His light
Will lead you on where He would have you go—
 If He but lead, thy pathway must be right.

And when by her earth's pilgrimage is done—
   When God has called her home to perfect rest—
Still will her teachings live, and you will know
   Of all God's earthly gifts her love was best.
You, too, will know that she is waiting where
God will you one day take, her bliss to share.

      *   *   *   *   *

Dear child, know this : 'Tis sent from Him above—
The precious gift of a True Mother's Love !

MY TREASURE.

("Bobbie," 1874.)

TWO large full eyes—loving, tender, and true —
With merriment beaming—of violet hue ;
Two little hands, only fitted for play,
Busy with mischief full half of the day :
Two little feet, that go tramping along.
Resting hardly a moment all day long.

Listening to things that they should not hear,
Two little ears injudiciously near ;
And these little matters to memory's hall
Two sweet little lips will often recall ;
One little body, whom mother all day
Must carefully watch, lest her boy should stray.

One minute climbing on table or chair,
The next he is hiding you know not where ;
Then there's a rush and a loving caress- -
A romp, and a hug full of tenderness—
Coaxing dear mother to tell him a tale,
To mend him his whip, or make him a sail.

Yet, tho' often mischievous, wayward, wild,
Full of love is ever my darling child ;
And when he comes, with affection's pure kiss,
To ask my pardon for deed done amiss,
I feel a mother's best, tenderest joy
In fondly forgiving my erring boy.

And when at eve he is tired of his play,
Washed ready for bed, he kneels down to pray,
With brown chubby hands clasped tightly in prayer,
I think of his future while watching there,
And often anxiously, earnestly pray
God to keep "My Treasure" in Wisdom's way.

Now he has kissed us all—"Good-night !"—at rest,
His curly head leaning on mother's breast—
My neck fondly circled with tiny arm —
I feel that to guard him safe from all harm
I can cheerfully all day's troubles bear,
For *pure love* repays a true mother's care.

ACROSTIC.

JULY 10TH, 1884.

C HILD, do you feel how solemn is the vow
O rdained for you to take upon this night?
N ow, think how fervently you then must pray
F or God's good grace to aid thee in the fight.
I n all temptations, dangers that beset,
R ight loyally do thou thy Master serve.
M ay never cowardice bid thee desert
A Saviour's side, or from His precepts swerve.
'T is not a form alone, though thoughtless minds,
I ndeed, may think 'tis but a rite of man.
O ! be it, child, to thee a means whereby
N ew grace is given to do the best you can.

 SIMPLE word here,
   A simple word there,
   Only a word on the way;
   Spoken in weakness,
   Spoken in meekness,
But growing in strength each day.

A simple word here,
A simple word there,
From those words what good will spring
   God alone can tell,
   But *He* knows full well
They will fruit to *His harvest* bring.

LINES GIVEN TO MY SON WITH A SILVER WATCH—1884.

O thee, my son, my Alexander dear,
I give this silver watch, with love sincere ;
You know that it is placed within your care,
Memento of affection. You will wear
It next your heart, and I trust you will prize
More than the watch—that which it tells thee flies—
The precious time that God to thee has given,
May you so spend 'twill make you meet for Heaven.
I know, most careful of the watch you'll be
Because thy mother's hand did give it thee ;
But, darling boy, more careful be to show
In all thy actions that God's grace you know ;
Much happier it will make thy mother's heart
To know her child doth choose "the better part "—
To know he prizes more the gifts of love
Sent from his Heavenly Father's house above
Than gifts of earth, however dear they be.
(The gifts of grace will last eternally !)
A pure, a thankful heart, an upright mind,
I pray be yours ; may you true wisdom find

Each day as time glides swiftly on its way—
Each week, each year, that God permits thee stay
This life to live—that while you this life know—
That while you do life's duties here below,
You may at all times feel your heart is strong
To do the right, to overcome the wrong!
I know temptations always will beset
These paths of earth ; but if you strive to get
Dominion over Satan's wiles and power,
You will o'ercome, in evil's trying hour—
O'ercome, thro' seeking strength from One above,
Who, though so just, is still a God of love.

     *   *   *   *   *

My boy, we know not what a day may bring!
And if too soon, for thee, upon Time's wing,
It should be I am called to leave thy side,
Remember well my counsels—still abide
Within the "narrow path" where day by day
I strove for years to lead thee on the way—
The way that leads to brighter home above,
Where all is harmony and perfect love.
And whilst I'm speaking, darling, thus to thee,
Some words I add—of these most mindful be—
The words are these : Thy younger brother dear,
Whom I have loved like thee for many a year,
Who, like thyself, by me is prized so well
That words would fail thy mother's love to tell :
Thy only brother, Robert, do thou guide
With best of brother's counsel ; by his side

Do thou be near in sorrow's trying time !
And, like my prayers have ofttimes mixed with
    thine,
So do thou daily let thy voices be
Upraised to Heaven ; upon thy bended knee
Do thou together ask thy God in prayer
To guide, protect, and keep thee everywhere ;
In duties, or in pleasures, or in woe,
That He be with thee wheresoe'er you go ;
For if you ask aright, be sure that He
Will guide, sustain, and help continually.
And may the bonds of brotherhood be such
Between my boys, that you may firmly trust
Each in the other—may you ever share
The other's joy and pleasure, pain or care.

    *   *   *   *   *

And when this changing life is ended here,
May you, my boys, within God's home appear ;
There meet again your father dear and I,
Where tears of parting no more dim the eye—
Where re-united on that brighter shore
We all will dwell with God for evermore.

A FABLE.

N ancient King (the fable runs)
 A message sent one day
Unto another olden King—
 The message this did say :
  "Send me a pig : I'd like it blue
(And mind do not delay)—
Its tail as black as ink must be,
 Or else"—he did not say
What else—or, if he had, perhaps
 A pig he would have got ;
But a blue pig with a black tail
 This rival King had not.
So this reply was quickly sent :
 " A good pig or a bad,
With blue skin and a tail like ink,
 I've not got. If I had——"
And just through this they went to war ;
 They laid their kingdoms bare.
Their armies, too, did they exhaust ;
 Their treasures, great and rare,
Were sacrificed through this small thing ;
 And when near all was lost,
They both thought they had foolish been
 To reckon not the cost.

12

They each began, at last, to wish
  Sweet peace they could restore ;
Ere this might be they must explain
  Unto each other more.
What first it was that made them start
  To fight one with another—
That hate they bear each one unto
  Instead of love like brother.
" What could you mean," the second King
  Unto the first did say,
" By saying, ' Send me a blue pig
  (And mind you don't delay)
With a black tail, or else'—else what
  I want of you to know.
Why did you such a message send—
  Such insult to me show ? "
Then answer made this first great King :
  " A blue pig did I mean,
With a black tail, you should me send
  (Whether 'twere fat or lean) ;
And if you had not such an one,
  I must do with another.
I put ' or else,' so you should know
  To send me any colour."
After the first King had explained
  What he so clearly meant,
Unto the other he did say—
  " That answer that you sent,
' I have not got one ; if I had—'
  That's what I could not bear.
Such words that you to me should use
  I really thought a care."

" Well," said the second King, "I can
   That very soon explain :
If pig I'd had, I should have sent
   It to you is quite plain."
The explanation then was done—
   Each King his folly saw ;
And firmer friends these Kings became
   Than e'er they were before.
This fable might to boys and girls
   A useful lesson teach,
That they, for trifling, small mistakes,
   Too often make a breach.
Too oft a thing misunderstood
   Will make one's friend a foe—
Will, when it should be full of joy,
   Make the heart throb with woe.
Oft quarrels quite as foolish are
   As war of the black pig ;
We wait not for each to explain,
   Our pride's so mighty big.
We draw conclusions far too fast—
   But one view do we take—
And thus, like kings of olden time,
   Oft make some great mistake.

STANZA.

HREE children of one household—they were all
That God had sent to bless that earthly home.
Three fair sweet flowers—with what devoted care
Each one was watched and tended ! Yet, with all
The love and tenderness which they knew here,
There was *A Friend* who loved those children more
Than even they to whom He had them sent.
He looked—He saw that they were tender lambs,
Unfit to battle with life's storms and cares,
And so He took them to a *Better Land.*

*   *   *   *   *

Poor mother ! crushed with grief ; poor father ! mourn
Not for thy dear ones—only for thy loss ;
For they are safe in God's own keeping, where
In after-time you will their glory share.

*   *   *   *   *

My heart aches for you both. I cannot say
In words the sympathy for thee I feel.
May He who gave, and He who took away,
Send solace from above—thy grief to heal.
No human friend can aid at such a time.
No human voice can consolation tell ;
But, oh ! may God Himself console and bless,
And whisper to thee : "*I do all things well !*"

October 2nd, 1885.

OUR ALICK.

1871.

UR own sweet Alick, our darling boy,
So full of innocence, love, and joy;
I think, when gazing on his fair face,
It is far too pure for earthly place—
It is more fitted for home above,
'Mid cherubs of spotless truth and love,
Than to be in world of grief and sin,
With cares without and troubles within.

*   *   *   *

I loved our boy with affection rare,
When first I felt a mother's fond care ;
And as I thanked my Father above
For gift sent to us in boundless love,
With my prayers were tears—I wept for joy—
That he was my own, my lovely boy.
But his winsome ways and prattle gay
Make me greater prize him day by day ;
And, watching him with a mother's pride,
I think no other like him beside.

*   *   *   *

I pray the Giver of all that is good
Preserve our Alick to reach manhood ;
May He direct him from early hours
To youth's bright age with golden flowers—
From youth to manhood his footsteps guide,
O'er all his pleasures and ways preside.

     *   *   *   *

Our darling boy ! may God's own good care
Protect and keep him everywhere.

AN ENIGMA.

Y first you'll find in seed, but not in sowing.
My second is in plant, but not in growing.
My third is in pleasure, but 'tis not in joy.
My fourth is in urchin, but never in boy.
My fifth is in lesson, but 'tis not in task.
My sixth is in cover, but absent from mask.
My whole is a plant : its blossoms do bear
An exquisite fragrance of perfume quite rare.

Answer—DAPHNE.

FRIENDS.

HEN I see the leaves down falling,
　　Soon as Autumn doth begin,
From the trees they firmly clung to
　　In the bright glad time of Spring,
　　Such I think is worldly friendship.
While abundance with us lasts
Friends (so called) will round us gather :
But when winter o'er us casts
Its dark shade of need or sorrow,
　　They no longer wish to stay—
Then, as leaves drop from their branches,
Untrue "*Friends*" all haste away.

ADVICE.

E do not often stumble
    Upon the roughest way,
Because we look where danger lies
    Before us day by day.

'Tis where the path is smoothest,
    Where even is the road,
That, by a little thing unseen,
    We fall beneath the load.

And so it is, dear children,
    With persons whom you meet ;
Oft those who speak too smoothly
    Are like to even street.

Where least you think are dangers,
    Temptations there may be,
So never be too trustful
    Of those who flatter thee.

Those friends who show you kindly,
    With truthful lip and heart,
The obstacles before you
    Along life's rugged path ;

Who tell you of your weakness,
    Your thoughtless faults reprove,
Are those that you should trust in—
    Are those whom you should love.

Like the road that is uneven—
    The road you walk with care—
True friends will always teach you
    Of life's dangers to beware.

So, if you take instruction,
    And follow what they tell,
Tho' duty's path seems hardest,
    You will do your duties well.

And when youthful years have gone,
    'Tis likely you may know
That, to friends did you reprove,
    Success in life you owe.

NEW YEAR CARD COUPLETS.

O-DAY another year is born for thee,
And with its birth may you new blessings see !

MAY every gift of love and joy
Be always thine without alloy !

For thee, dear friend, with heart sincere,
I wish a happy, bright New Year !

MAY love and joy for thee with years increase,
Thy life be filled with good—its end be peace !

THE seasons change ; but may true love for thee
Be changeless as the seasons changing be !

OD bless you !—keep you in His way
Each year, each month, each week, each day ;
And when for thee brief *Time* is done,
May glad *Eternity* be won !

SCRAPS AND COUPLETS.

SCRAPS AND COUPLETS.

BIRTHDAY.

 ANY happy returns !—the old, old lay
  send to thee, my friend, with love to-
  day ;
With these I send a warm and true caress,
And trust that priceless joys thee ever
bless.

WE waft our loving thoughts to-day,
  We pray that God may bless,
A friend to whom we owe far more
Than words can well express.

TRUE friends are rare—know how to prize them.

BE true in all things—let men see
Your words and actions well agree.

A wise friend points to our errors.

———

Try to be wise, and learn to know
That silence oft doth wisdom show.

———

Within their hearts, how many bear
A secret sorrow—a hidden care!

———

It is better to be silent than to speak unkindly truths.

———

Gold never yet hath won esteem—
It oft has bought it, well I ween.

———

A kindness done in time of necessity is one that can never be fully repaid.

———

He who spends his life as his life should be spent,
Will have little time to waste in discontent.

———

How little minds do like to show their power!

———

The sun did never shine without it cast a shade.

———

Deceit in friendship is the basest kind.

HE who is slow to promise what you ask,
Will be most likely to fulfil the task.

NEVER forget one who has been your friend.

CHARITY and Justice are two good proofs of Christianity.

FEW deeds are lost.   If courtesy you show,
Through acts of same you may true friendship know.

HE who imputes wrong motives is to himself no friend ;
Grieve not though, with such a man, thy friendship hath
an end.

BE courteous, truthful, kind, and just.

WE all alike, within this " vale of tears,"
Find pleasure mixed with pain, and hopes with fears.

GOD gives us dear ones for to prize and love ;
He takes them for to lift our hearts above.

KEEP smiles for the world ;
Let your tears be seen only by a friend.

IF pure the heart that you do once deceive,
Though truth you tell, it will not truth believe.

13

OTHERS know not our sorrow; so likewise we know not the sorrow of others.

THEY say oft stupids good work criticise,
Let such do better for to teach the wise.

SEEK not to call a man or woman friend,
Unless, through good or ill, you will defend.

THOUGH others be unjust, let us be kind;
Such charity doth show a Christian mind.

TRUE friendship is a thing wealth cannot buy,
For friends by riches made with riches fly.

LET not the fear of ridicule cause you to deny your principle.

OF women mealy-mouthed be thou afraid;
Such women mischief make on land or wave.

ONE good rule of life is to never let anyone do for us that which we can do for ourselves.

IT is the little things of life
That ofttimes bring us care and strife.

He that giveth thee wise counsel is a good friend

We all have sorrows that the world knows not ;
Unclouded joys can here be no man's lot.

There is no doubt *experience* teaches.   We also know
life is full of lessons.

Always try to do your best.

A good book is a desirable companion.

What magic power true friendship can impart !
It joy increaseth, cheers the wounded heart.

Let *faith*, and *hope*, and *charity* be thine.

" What might have been " 'tis not for us to say ;
What is, is God's will, and we must obey.

Any way that is always smooth is not the right way.

It matters not the church or creed you own,
So that with fear you serve your God alone.

I know what has been, I know what is, but I know
not what is to come.

ALWAYS be proud, but let your pride be seen
In truth and goodness, and in noble mien.

LET us give to others pleasure ; in doing so we are sure
to find it ourselves.

No one but God can us the future tell ;
Leave it to Him, and know all will be well.

LOOK on the cheerful side of life, and see
That flowers bloom there for thee continually.

Or,

IF you would rather cross the way, and find
The sharpest thorns, have discontented mind.

THREE things worth having—a cheerful heart, a cheerful fire, and a cheerful friend.

THE best cure for dulness is to find some occupation.

IT is better to be deceived than to be suspicious.

IF you would noble be, seek not to please
The world alone, but give thy conscience ease.

NEVER neglect an opportunity of doing good.

A LIFE of self-indulgence and of ease
Is not the life a noble mind to please.

———

A MAN who will fearlessly speak his mind, even against
his own interest, is a man whom you can trust.

———

JUDGE not another ; bear in mind
One *Judge* there is for all mankind.

———

EVERY man or woman can do something to contribute
to the happiness of others.

———

To work and do one's duty
Shows nobleness and worth.

———

CHARITY will cover, but true modesty will prevent,
many sins.

———

THERE is no use disputing with a man you know
you'll not convince, say all you can.

———

AN open-hearted man is generally a sincere one.

———

GOOD nature, with good sense and virtue, hold—
You will be rich, though small your stock of gold.

———

'TIS better to have a humble joy than know a golden
sorrow.

DESPISE a slander—it will die ;
Refute it—it will right a lie.

———

IF hate you plant to-day, be sure to-morrow
The growth of same will bring you bitter sorrow.

———

To start in time is better than to run
When only half our journey we have done.

———

THOSE who will wound the sorrowful and poor
Will cringe immensely at the rich man's door.

———

No place on earth like *home*, where home is blest
With pure affections from unselfish breast.

———

ALL lives will bring forth either weeds or flowers.

———

A MAN'S actions that are seen
Will tell the virtues are within.

———

SELF-RELIANCE will generally dispel discontent.

———

'TIS wise to scorn the weakness of one's self,
'Tis wise to blame the sins that we commit,
And thereby gain instruction how to act
In future, to avoid regretted faults.

CONTENTMENT is a source of wealth
That riches cannot buy.

WITH helping hand let sympathy be seen.

SMILES are to human beings what sunshine is to flowers.

IF we scatter seeds of blessing,
From the seeds will blessings spring.

IT is not the absence of temptation, but overcoming when one is tempted, that shows a man or woman's real character.

THERE is no use to vex ourselves for things we cannot help.

HE who is suspicious of other men should be suspected by those of whom he is suspicious.

THIS life, at best, is not all joy.

LET each one his own business mind,
And leave his friend's alone.

DO not let trifles prevent you from trying to achieve success.

SPEND well the present, and you may depend
The future you will find a worthy friend.

IF peace and quietness you would obtain,
A thousand things forget the same to gain.

LOOK not to find a friend without a fault;
Not faultless we who try that friend to find.

O FATHER! grant, on brightest shore,
We meet again to part no more!

ONE Friend I know a Friend will be
Through *time* and through eternity.

DEAL gently with the children : they will know,
When past is childhood, quite enough of woe.

To do one's duty cheerfully is to spend life well.

AN envious man hath trouble much to bear;
For others' joy will only bring him care.

MY son! remember, no one has the power
To rob you of good name, if so you live
That you deserve it.

ONE thought consoles us for this life's short space,
That time cannot eternity efface.

—————

HE who would safely rule, must rule in love.

—————

IT matters not the gain deceit obtains—
It only cheats the getter for his pains.

—————

TRUE friendship requires no ceremony.

—————

WHO will not reason must a bigot be ;
Who cannot, stupid is ;
And he who dares not; he must be a slave.

—————

WOULD'ST thou acquire wisdom ?
Thou must know life's disappointments.

—————

REMEMBER, he is powerful who can
Control his passions like a noble man.

—————

IF well you do the smallest thing, it is better than the
greatest not well done.

—————

'TIS far more easy some men to obey
Than others to command.

—————

THOSE who parade misfortune feel it least.

14

Write, talk, and think of virtue, if you will ;
But practise it—that will be better still.

Can'st thou judge another's heart
If you do not know your own ?

It is not always possible to keep from having
disagreeable things said of you, but you can always
keep from saying them of others.

God knows the cross that each the best can bear.

'Tis better for to think and not to speak,
Than for to speak and not think what we say.

Life has no business with you,
If you can nothing find to do.

While memory lives there are three things to which
the mind will often revert—a father's love, a mother's
care, and our childhood's home.

Each one is sent into this world
An appointed task to do.

Adversities, we often find,
Are blessings in disguise.

Is there a heart without its necropolis,
Where gravestone of its loved, its unforgotten, be.

CHRISTMAS DAY.

If you would Christians be, as Christians pray—
Forgive and kindly think of all to-day.

THE END.

George Robertson and Company, Printers, Melbourne.